ALL THE WAY TO ITA

All the Way to Italy
A tale of homecoming through generations past
by Flavia Brunetti

Illustrations: Cinzia Bolognesi
Internal graphic design and layout: Sara Calmosi

Ali Ribelli Edizioni
Women's Fiction

Ali Ribelli Edizioni
Via Bachelet 7b, Gaeta (LT)
04024
Italy
www.aliribelli.com – redazione@aliribelli.com

ISBN 978-88-33460-58-1

Printed in Italy.

ALL THE WAY TO ITALY

A tale of homecoming through generations past

by Flavia Brunetti

AliRibelli

To my aunties, Letizia e Giovanna.
Words, for once, would not suffice.
You raised me to keep the dance in my heart
and the iron in my backbone.
When I have not had the strength,
you have always stood for me.
I wish I could celebrate you both
in manners as fierce and regal as you take on life:
to write your names on the wings of the birds
that spiral the highest on feathers and hope,
for sphinxes to create riddles in your honor,
for tornadoes to dance to the rhythms of your words.
This book is for you; as humble a gift as any,
but you both know,
the one I always hoped to give you.

Contents

Firenze

Orvieto

Roma

Tivoli

Napoli

Sperlonga

Words can be worrisome, people complex,
motives and manners unclear,
Grant her the wisdom to choose her path right,
free from unkindness and fear.

Let her tell stories and dance in the rain,
somersault, tumble and run,
Her joys must be high as her sorrows are deep.
Let her grow like a weed in the sun.

Ladies of paradox, ladies of measure,
ladies of shadows that fall,
This is a prayer for a blueberry girl.
Words written clear on a wall.

Help her to help herself, help her to stand,
help her to lose and to find.
Teach her we're only as big as our dreams.
Show her that fortune is blind.

Truth is a thing she must find for herself,
precious and rare as a pearl.
Give her all these and a little bit more:
Gifts for a blueberry girl.

Blueberry Girl, Neil Gaiman

TRAVELS BACK

What if when you step on a plane
All the promises you made line up politely on the wings
And the only ones that survive
Are the ones you still remember on the other side?

Chapter 1
Present day.

Little was leaving home, but also, she supposed, she was returning home. She was settled as comfortably as possible, lost in thought, her face pressed to the window while the engine rumbled underneath her feet. Lost in thought was a phrase that could often describe Little, and just now she was wondering why it was necessary for a plane to be so cold. She supposed that there were all sorts of logical reasons for keeping humans at nearly subzero temperatures, squashed this many miles in the air, but she couldn't hear anything over the constant thrum of the air-conditioning, and she also hadn't been able to feel her toes for the last two hours.

Glancing at the austere businessman next to her, she was also thinking that planes were simultaneously wonderful and wretched creatures. *All of us locked in together*, she thought, *while knowing nothing about each other*. Who was the man going to greet when he arrived? Whom had he just said goodbye to? How did the city they were both going to tie them together, and, more importantly to Little—who had wept so copiously when departing San Francisco that her nose was still bright red—did they both love the city they had just left? She wanted to tap the man's shoulder and ask him if a place can ever shake off the people who had belonged to it, or if those tendrils would feed her nostalgia forever, for the rest of her life, which in that moment felt like it could be hundreds of years. It was then that the man noticed Little distractedly gazing at him and looked at her curiously. Maybe she should just write her thoughts down in her notebook, she considered, and let the man get on with his preferred onboard flight entertainment. At the moment, it appeared to be scratching at his nose.

Her name wasn't really Little, of course. Her father had started calling her that when she was small, before she had much of a choice, because she was the youngest. The name had stuck until everybody called her that, and she didn't mind, not really, since it had come from him. She frowned slightly in her seat in the middle of the sky and forced her thoughts to something else. She did not want to cry, so she rearranged her face and turned to the clouds outside.

"So, what takes you to Munich?" The deep voice startled her, and she turned back to the man, surprised that he had spoken so far into the flight. The rules of whether or not they would be the chatty type of seatmates should have already been set.

"Oh, I'm not staying in Munich. I'm going on to Rome." *Here it goes. Now he's going to tell me about his trips to Italy.*

"You don't say! Is this your first time? I've spent lots of time in Italy. Great place, great place. If you need any tips, you just let me know. Been there lots of times with the wife myself." He peered at her with interest.

"Oh, how lovely," she said, flinching at how insincere she sounded. "Not my first time, though, I'm actually going home. I'm from Rome."

"Really! How come you speak English so well? You sound just like an American!" This reaction always made Little feel even more of an impostor in the culture.

"I grew up studying in the States. I'm going home to be with my family because my father passed away."

The real story was that though Little was a card-carrying Italian (or Roman, as she had been raised always to say—Italians seemed to consider themselves by nationality and not by region only when Italy was playing in the World Cup), she barely considered herself one. When she had been a little Little, her father had sent her on a trip to San Francisco with his sister, who had been living there for years. Once ensconced in her Aunty Sira's world, Little had never wanted to return to Italy. And so she had spent her childhood and the majority of her teenage years growing up

2

in California, only seeing Rome on occasional summer holidays. She had liked it that way, had thought it would stay so forever.

"So, you're going back to stay?" the man asked.

"Yes," she said, deciding on impulse that there was no reason to explain the whole story to a stranger.

"Well, that'll be just lovely. Sorry to hear about your father."

Little tried not to grimace back, her hand instinctively reaching for the safety of the notebook in the seat pocket in front of her, flipping it open to the first blank page, only to find she had nothing to write. As was becoming increasingly the case, there was only silence.

She began to flip through the pages for inspiration, finding the beginning of a letter to Sira, one that had never gotten past the first line: Zia, I've lost my words. One page before that was the scribbled list she had made out a few days before, the one of things she wanted to remind herself about Sira. Sira, who had always baffled her, protected her, raised her without question. She looked at the list, smiling to herself, thinking of the tidbits of guidance that Sira threw out while she waved a kitchen spoon around, or picked out a pair of shoes, or walked the dog. Offering advice that she had carefully garnered throughout her long life was how she protected those she loved, padding their lives with the things she wished she had known herself. Little had always listened, because she found Sira's stories enthralling, but as she grew up, she realized more and more the worth and soundness of what her aunt had shared with her. Little scribbled a title on the top of the page: Top Ten Points You'll Hear Most Often If You Grew Up With Sira.

"So! When was the last time you were in Italy?" The man had started to speak again. She thought for a moment.

"About two years ago," she answered. After her father had succumbed to the cancer in his lungs and she, eighteen years old, an adult, had boarded the first plane she could get a seat on just days after the funeral.

"Quite a long time!" he crowed.

"It's been… " She was looking for a word to express what it had been, and came up with nothing. One morning during the year she was seventeen, Sira had walked into Little's bedroom in San Francisco and told her that

3

they needed to go home. Little had been confused for a moment about what she meant, and if she had known what Sira would say next, maybe she would have held her ears and closed her eyes. She would have forced the world to stay in that moment where she was sure that home was where she stood. Where she could place everyone that she loved in the certainty that the pieces were falling the way they were meant to.

But it had turned out that wasn't how cancer worked, and so they had left Northern California together. They left the place where they were both safely at home with every turn of the sycamores, and returned to a place Little barely knew, so that she could help a man she also barely knew die. Then she had run back to San Francisco under her student visa, started college there, and tried to pretend she had never left. Sira had stayed in Italy.

A few months after the funeral, which she tried her hardest to never ever consider, she began to notice that she was losing her words. Little had always written things down, had found a cauldron of words at her disposal when she had a pen in her hand, even when her shyness made it difficult to express herself out loud. It had always been so easy. Then, slowly, came an uncomfortable realization born of continual frustration at not being able to find the right expression in her writing. She disliked needing to repeat herself, to employ fallback words more and more often. She worried about the sieve. Now she no longer felt the urge to write stories or jot down a summary for herself, whether at the end of an ordinary day or because of a thought she wanted to remember. She didn't want to remember, anyway. She had realized then that something inside of her was making sure she knew she had made a mistake, that even though she could physically run away, she would still have to face herself.

Still, Little was convinced she could have borne it and pushed through until it had all meshed into something logical. She would have been able to move forward, forgetting about lingering family drama and old-fashioned Italy. She would have stayed in San Francisco. She fit there, felt modern and brand new. She was building something for herself that was the opposite of antiquated, a life that had nothing to do with anything before it. If she hadn't found what she had found. If she was one of those people who could leave well enough alone.

She excused herself to her seatmate, who was now flipping through the channels on the little screen in front of him, and walked to the bathroom. With the door locked, she turned to face the mirror. Wide, scared, dark brown eyes stared back at her reflection, and she suddenly missed Sira violently. *You'll see her in a few hours*, she said to herself, watching the words form on her lips as she pressed her hands against the mirror and leaned into herself.

Why does a memory matter? Little thought now, frowning at her own reflection. *Why do I need to know what I'm missing?* She wished planes could reverse.

When the plane set its wheels down in Munich several hours later, the thin businessman (was he a businessman? Little realized she had never even asked) turned to her and shook her hand formally.

"Good luck, then." He smiled, but was not paying real attention. His mind was already collecting his luggage, leaving the airport, calling a cab.

"Thank you," Little replied graciously; and only once the plane had settled on the landing strip and the man had left his seat did she finish quietly, "I wish I could be sure that luck was all I needed."

Top Ten Points You'll Hear Most Often If You Grew Up With Sira (Or, How to Survive Life)

I. Never put a comma where you should put a period. I'm not talking about grammar, kiddo.

II. If any part of your body or soul hurts, it's because *hai preso un colpo d'aria*—essentially, you got hit by some air. You got air-punched. Somehow, somewhere, cold air blew on you and that's why your lower back/throat/chest/ankle hurts. Seriously. Generations of Italian grandmothers before me have believed this, and this is why we bundle our children and our children's children like fat little snowmen even though the sun is singing its victory outside. Go put some sunglasses on over that scarf.

III. No matter what the weather looks like, it's cold. Bring an umbrella. What do you mean it's August? When you come back in the house in an hour drenched, don't complain to me that your new boots aren't waterproof, sweetheart.

IV. If something breaks, don't fix it. Get a new one. Nothing is irreplaceable, and gluing it back together is just your way of not being able to let it go. Things glued back together will always break along the same lines. You're stronger than that. I'm not talking about vases here, either.

V. Shoulders back. Head up. Always. Even when you are alone. Especially when you are alone.

VI. As long as your hair looks great and you have nice shoes, you can get away with anything.

6

VII. People tend to not be as smart as they think they are. You tend to be smarter than you think you are. But don't be so naïve about it.

VIII. If I were your age, I would be wreaking havoc all over this town. Have a little courage. You can wear that color now, you won't be able to wear it when you're fifty—well, you will, but you'll look stupid.

IX. You can do anything. You can do everything. Stop being so scared, stop settling, and *stop* comparing yourself to everybody else. If you're going to settle down I want it to be because it's absolutely the best that you could ever want for yourself, not because you're *worried* that it's the best you'll ever be able to get for yourself.

X. There is absolutely no point to nude eyeshadow.

Chapter 2
Rome, Italy. Present day.

Little was trying to get a good look at Sira out of the corner of her eye; she needed an idea of what the older woman might be feeling. There had been a time when they lived in almost total symbiosis, when Little could tell how Sira felt by the arch of her eyebrow, the way she outlined the bones of her jaw with an index finger when she was annoyed. She could feel nothing now. She was too tired and too far out of her element.

She contented herself with watching her aunt as she busied about the kitchen, making *brodo* as their family always did when someone came in from a long journey. The homemade broth made from chicken stock was so revered in the Italian countryside that Little had believed for years growing up that it was the reverently spooned-out *brodo* that had nursed her back to health after bad bouts with the flu. Sira had tried to teach her how to use *odori* to spice the broth, the "scents" given away at local markets that would spice a dish, give it flavor. Carrots, celery, rosemary, and what else?

Sira was slight in her old age but still as beautiful as a statue, her dignity draped over her like a gossamer shawl, paired with still-brilliant eyes and an unwavering, unapologetic gaze. The world and the way that it passed inside of her had caused her beauty to become more pronounced. She was warier, sharper. Those who knew Sira knew that she had never cared much for her looks but had invested, deeply, in her mind. She had passed this trait on to the children she had raised, both the one that was her own and the one that she had raised for her brother.

"You're blonde now?" Sira began, and Little was grateful that she hadn't had to speak first.

"Yep," she replied, pulling at a lock of travel-worn hair and glancing at the frizz with a sigh. Her hair never cooperated in general, much less after traveling. She pushed it back into a semblance of neatness.

"It's a thing," she said.

Sira grinned. "You know what I was thinking the other day?" she said, stirring the liquid in the pot lightly. "About the way you write your little sentences at the end of things. Little captions. Do you still do that?"

Little's smile was lopsided. "Yeah, zia, of course I do." She had a feeling that it would upset Sira to tell her that she hadn't had the heart to write much in the past few years.

"Sometimes they didn't seem to have much to do with what had happened, but it was what came out for you. A form of digestion, a release." Sira was smiling at her now, reminiscing, and Little remembered suddenly that though she had always been unreasonably private about these snippets of her world, she had always read them eagerly to Sira. Sira always listened.

"So," Sira said, turning away from the stovetop, "how is San Francisco?"

"It's great." Her mind traveled back to her last stroll through the city, walking up the steep steps of Lyon Street to the breathtaking view at the end; how every time the vista was somehow different, the light playing on something new to see. Something she had somehow missed the times before. Had she really been there only a day ago? "There's always something to do, somewhere to go, and I love school, even though the classes are hard."

"You don't mind studying political science?" asked Sira, standing at the sink.

Little had always wanted to study literature or creative writing, subjects her father had frowned upon. He thought that a college degree should be sensible, something she could fall back on, and that the creativity could come on the side.

"I don't, actually. This way I get to learn about stuff I don't know about, something different from what I tend to lean toward. And," she said, shifting forward in her seat in excitement, "I get to take literature courses on the side as electives, and I just finished an awesome psych course, so I think I want to take more of those."

Sira was looking fixedly at the pot again, and Little realized she should address Sira's request, the phone call she had made to Little a few weeks prior. Come home.

"I looked at some of the courses offered by the Political Science department at the Italian university here, and I've also been talking to one of the American universities in the center. I have my transcripts with me." She was working hard to sound upbeat, confident. "So, either way, if I decide to stay after the summer, I'll be set to start something here by September. It's only May, so I have the whole summer to figure things out."

"That sounds like a good plan!" Sira sounded relieved. "What about your apartment?" She began rummaging around in the refrigerator, pulling out various bits of vegetables.

"Aleth said she doesn't mind living there alone for the summer, and then if I decide not to go back she'll get a new roommate in the fall."

Sira nodded. "Are you in touch with any of your old friends from here?"

"A few. Mostly Barbara."

"That nice blonde girl that used to spend the summers at the house across the street from ours in Sperlonga?"

"That's the one."

"Well, it'll be nice to see her," Sira ventured. Little nodded slowly. "Get you used to being home."

"I feel like I left home yesterday," she blurted out, almost without meaning to. She had promised herself that if she agreed to her aunt's request to return to Italy, she was going to stick to it without complaining, at least through the summer. But almost immediately the smells and colors of Rome had felt shrill and unreal to her, even in the twilight of her cab ride to the apartment. She needed to say something to alleviate the pressure building inside of her. Sira turned. She suddenly looked her age, and Little felt a thrill of fear at remembering that Sira was not, after all, immortal.

"You know how that feels?" she tried, looking up at her aunt.

"Yes. I do know." Sira brushed her hand lightly against her niece's flushed cheek. "You look so tired, Little, and you've come so many miles. I know that trip always wore me down to the bone. Maybe you should get some rest."

Little leaned her cheek into her aunt's open hand. Sira smiled, her green eyes crinkling. "Welcome back, *piccola*."

***

She woke with a start in the dark room in what felt like the stark middle of the night. She vaulted almost all the way out of the bed before remembering where she was. Rome. Her father's apartment. Her apartment now, her sleep-addled brain reminded her, and this cut through the fog of her dream. *I don't want it*, she thought. *Bring him back, I don't want it, he can have it back.* She tried to close her eyes again and conjure an image of something that normally helped her find rest, like a deeper point of sea off the island of Ponza or the view of the bay from the Tiburon pier, but her heartbeat did not slow down. With a sigh she opened her eyes again and looked out the window.

She had insisted on sleeping with the window shutters thrown completely open, although Sira had disagreed. Rome was not as safe a city as it once was, she argued, and they were on the ground floor. Then she had taken one look at her claustrophobic niece and helped her to open the window as far as it would go.

Now Little could see what she hadn't paid attention to in her earlier exhaustion. The high rise of the immortal Aurelian Walls carpeted the view before her, the protective rings of stone that delineated the ancient city of Rome. She had grown up with this view. Now it felt even more etched by time, and unfamiliar. Her fingers smarting, Little realized she had scratched her left hand, her writing hand, while she dreamt.

The dream had started comfortably enough, in gray, which she did not mind. For many years, her sleeping self had harbored and nested these tinctures, the husky brown, clay tan, musky half-pigments. Then an unsettling dream event had occurred, colors flooding everywhere: fuchsia gushing from her fingers, vibrant turquoise leaping from her neck, chartreuse twining down her legs and mixing with spreading citrine. Her fingerprints left behind halos of chrome, and when she began to cry her tears flowed violet, lavender, lemon. She had turned away to deny them, and to her horror they had only grown more fiercely vibrant. She had burst into a violent run, only to find gold and tangerine footprints scattering in her wake. Alone in a clear blue night, her heart had swelled suddenly with the joy of her hues, and she thought that maybe she knew what she could do with them. But the dream had again taken a turn, and she felt as though she were on a high ledge preparing for a great leap, the sensation of isolation sharp in her gut. She had backtracked to safety, and when her heel had hit the edge of something sharp she had awoken, the pads of her fingers brushing the air. Staring up at the ceiling, not yet fully awake, she somehow knew that if her dream self had leapt, her wings would have unfurled, and she would have found a tempest of colors tattooed on feathers that would have granted her flight. She had a fleeting vision of what it would have looked like, a minute plunge before a bursting rise.

Little looked out the window at the soft glow of the Aureliane as they stood the same guard they had stood for thousands of years, feeling uncomfortable and afraid. She never felt like this at home, never had chimerical dreams, never felt like her heart was exploding out of her chest. At home? She had to leave this city.

Chapter 3
San Francisco, California. Three months earlier.

There had been two things. One had happened late at night and was so seemingly random that Little still wasn't sure why she had attributed any importance to it. She had been sitting on the couch in the San Francisco apartment she shared with her best friend, Aleth, dozing lightly while a documentary played itself out on the television. It was on World War II, a subject she tended not to pay too much attention to because she'd heard about it so often. Sira and Enrico had been children during the war, and it had often been the backdrop of the stories Sira had told Little growing up. The few times she'd asked her dad about his own wartime memories, he had laughed and told her it was a good rule not to make memories back then, that he'd been young, and that bombs and hunger weren't much worth remembering.

The television was flashing pictures in black and white, slow reels of old recordings, mostly soldiers. An image flickered onto the screen, an ornate symbol engraved onto a wall of what looked like a bundle of sticks tied together with an ax emerging from the center. The image had sped by but Little leaned in closer, suddenly awake, groping for the remote before remembering she couldn't rewind normal television.

"Hey, Aleth, hey," she said, kicking out a foot to awaken her sleeping friend from the other side of the couch, "did you see that?"

"What? No, Little, I'm mostly asleep, what's up?" Aleth mumbled from her cocoon of covers.

"I know that symbol. I think I've seen it before," Little said, attention now fully focused on the presenter who had strolled onto a stage on the screen.

"Yes, well, that's World War II, no? We've all seen all of that stuff before," Aleth replied, wriggling out of her blankets and setting her feet down on the floor. "Terrible, tragic, all of it. Can we watch something happier? Want some popcorn?" She tugged on her socks and walked out of the living room. Little flicked off the set and got up to follow her friend into the kitchen, wondering why the image had made her think suddenly of her dead father, as though he were still around to ask questions to.

That would have been that, if Little hadn't thought to mention it to Sira the next day during their weekly (or biweekly, thought Little guiltily as she typed the Italian country code into her phone) call.

"It felt like something that I should recognize, like there was something I'm not quite getting," she said into the phone, lying on the couch and swinging her feet.

"Well, you're probably just tired from school. Best not to get caught up in those documentaries late at night," Sira replied vaguely without asking for more details. It was so unlike her that Little had been tempted to probe further before realizing she had no reason to and had shrugged the whole thing off.

The second thing had happened a few weeks later, when Little had come home to piles of papers on the floor and Aleth lugging boxes around.

"We are cleaning out our lives," huffed Aleth as she picked up a box stuffed full of what looked like her old coursework. "Self-improving. You know." She pointed to a small pile at the end of the hallway. "That's the stuff you brought back with you from Italy two years ago. I didn't want to throw it out, but, *two years*. I will make some tea and we can sort," she continued as she dropped another box onto the floor. "A new semester is coming up, we need to... "

"Self-improve?" Little grinned at Aleth, whose cheerfulness seemed ever-present, always close to the surface. It was one of the reasons Little enjoyed living with her. Aleth nodded vigorously, scooping up Little's papers and waving them over her head.

16

"Get to it!"

Little had been half-heartedly going through what appeared to be old medical records, wondering why on earth she had grabbed those papers from her father's apartment in Rome after his funeral, why it had seemed so important to keep something, anything, of his with her, when a single folded piece of paper had drifted onto her lap. She picked it up absentmindedly, smoothing out the old creases, munching on a biscuit as she did so. The chewing slowly stopped as she read the short, typewritten message again.

thought you'd leave. And if you've decided this, then I have only one request to make. If you do not love me enough, Delila, and maybe I have not earned your love, maybe my deceit was severe enough to cost me your love (and I do not blame you for this, and, as you asked, I will not tarnish your memory of your own father in hopes of restoring myself with you), then I beg of you, I implore you not to allow this to take away your love for your daughter. She must not pay the price for this. She is so very small, and

Little's heart sank all the way to her feet and continued through the floor. She flipped the paper over, already knowing there was nothing on the back, that the page was a part of a longer message, though a quick rifle through the rest of the mess on the table revealed no partner page.

"What are you doing?" asked Aleth, eyeing Little's sweeping motions across the mahogany table as they caused several papers to swoosh onto the floor.

"This," said Little, now picking pages up seemingly at random and dropping them again haphazardly, "is part of a letter. And it mentions my mother."

"Your mysterious mother!" said Aleth, reaching out to pluck the note from Little's hands. "May I? Who do you think wrote it?"

"My dad, I suppose," shrugged Little, who was beginning to feel vaguely numb. "Unless this is from Delila's papers, and someone else wrote it to her, but I think… " she frowned because she did not know what else to do, "I think it's my father, and he's talking about me."

"This is like something out of a mystery book," murmured Aleth, who was a big fan of the genre, as she read the note. "You should definitely ask Sira about this, Little."

"Zia does not love talking about Delila. She starts skirting the issue, which is weird because she's one of those head-on people, you know…" Little suddenly paused as she remembered the conversation she had had with her aunt a few weeks before. "But, when she doesn't want to talk about something, she pretends it doesn't exist. And honestly, Aleth, I don't push it because it upsets her, and I never really worked out the whole thing anyway, and it's probably best left alone." She turned to look at Aleth, whose focus was still trained on the letter in her hand.

"That is definitely the way things gets sorted out in a detective novel, and also in real life. Everyone just ignores it, and it goes away." She gave Little a meaningful look before moving to the phone as it rang, picking up the handset and checking the Caller ID before throwing it to Little. "Italy," she said with a wicked grin before heading out of the kitchen, "what timing! I told you this is just like a good Agatha Christie! Wait, no, people always die in Agatha Christies… I'll have to think of another comparison… "

Little brought the phone to her ear while her friend's voice faded down the hallway, mentally calculating whether it was worth it to mention Delila, her estranged mother whom they never discussed. Should she bring up the symbol again? Definitely unrelated, she knew, but it was all still stirring up old feelings in her mind that she connected to her old life, thoughts she preferred not to linger over. It was the reason she hadn't Googled the stupid symbol, though her fingers had hovered over the keyboard. *It doesn't matter, Little. Leave it alone.*

"Little?" Sira's voice wafted over the phone, always a little bit louder than it needed to be, as Sira did not trust anything over long distances except for paper and pen.

"*Ciao, zia, che c'è?*" It was unlike Sira to call in the middle of the week.

"I was thinking, after we talked last week."

"Yeah?" Little's eyes drifted to the open letter on the kitchen table. Maybe she could ask.

"I've been wanting to talk to you for some time, anyway. There are some things to resolve, here at home, things your father left behind." Little began to fidget, uncomfortable. This was a conversation *she* had been avoiding. "Isn't it about time you came home, Little?"

18

Chapter 4
Rome. Present day.

Rome was washed clean today, and Little took it as a sign that she could not hide forever. Dawn had come early, as it did in May, and remembering how spring paid homage to this city, she decided the jet lag was not worth staying hunched under the blankets.

Sometimes Rome was everybody's: the historians, the tourists, the archaeologists, the Italians. And not just every*body*, but every *time*. The city was precariously perched, its relationship with ticking moments insubstantial; its centuries past were as important, and seemingly more decisive, than its present. Rome was diaphanous, abstract. What Little set out for that morning was a chance to introduce herself to it again before the day was in full swing, while there was no one in the cobbled streets and the city could still recognize her.

She headed for the place that lay between the Aventine and Palatine Hills, where she used to go running, which was once the chariot racing stadium of the ancient Romans. It was the site that dictated how games would be played for the civilization that created it and for those that came afterward. Early morning light flung itself everywhere, as though in celebration of the terra-cotta walls lining the road and the feisty green of the trees that always surprised Little in their abundance.

Automatically her mind counted back to what time it would be in California. Nine p.m. What were her friends doing? What would she be doing if she were there? She'd had a part-time job after class at a real estate firm, which paid her well to draft and edit their documents and review their accounts. She was terrible at the accounting part but did so well when they needed editing or a description of a property written up that they had dubbed her "the comma monster" and treated her like a full-time member of the team.

She didn't realize that her feet were pulling her on their own, treading the path they still remembered. In her mind she was thousands of miles away, walking down different streets with different names and a different purpose. Only when she arrived at her destination did her mind return to Rome: Little had come back to Circus Maximus.

She sat on the top step that began the way to the park below, dizzy from having come back so many miles so quickly; she had, after all, been in San Francisco just a moment ago, and the rust red of the Golden Gate was still hovering on the edges of her vision. She was facing the Palatine Hill, one of her favorite views of the city, with its ruins of the House of Augustus, which Caesar Augustus had called home once he had founded the Roman Empire. Little wanted to think that they weren't that grand-looking after all, but the truth was that they took her breath away. These ruins wore their grandeur like silk, and Little, who loved language more than she cared to admit, could not help but think of the way this place, that she was in the presence of this very moment, had affected modern English. She remembered her father taking her here, putting his hands on her shoulders and turning her gently so that she faced the direction of the high, crumbling walls.

"Palatino, Little. That's where the word palace comes from. And Augustus? August! Is that not, what's that word you use, cool? Really cool? Just a little old empire, and we're still speaking it today."

And she had rolled her eyes. She remembered now, even though she had tried for two years not to. She thought she might be able to handle entire decades of not remembering, if only given the chance. How the shock of the funeral didn't reverberate for entire days afterward, until one afternoon when she took out her phone to call him, scrolled down to his number, and realized that the number went nowhere. She had called anyway, letting it ring and ring (had no one turned it off?), and finally the answering machine had clicked into gear. Although she thought she should hang up in horror, she instead felt herself pressing the phone to her ear harder, clinging to the sound of his voice. She had cried then, finally, standing in the middle of Circus Maximus, surrounded by the daunting history that her father had adored and she had so disdained.

Watching a gull soar slowly over the concave opening that was the Circus today, and an early determined jogger make his way across it, for the first time in a long time Little let herself not forget.

She had been a little girl, back in Rome for the holidays, and she was running after her father as he strode through Piazza Navona, excitedly pointing out to her the masterpieces of Bernini and Della Porta. She had not been interested, had already been counting down the days before she would go back to San Francisco. He had eyed her, and when she met his gaze, it was so observant that it made her look away. She had always found him larger than life, sweet but always a bit frightening, and she did not like to think that he was not impressed by her.

Uncomfortable in a world of marble and ruins and stories of murdered rulers, and angry that he assumed that she belonged here, she had announced that none of it mattered to her. She was a Californian, and she never intended to live here. Not ever. She had been surprised and even more perturbed when he had laughed openly, throwing his head back.

"You still don't know Rome, little one. You don't know how the *città* runs in your blood." He had always been dramatic, and mellifluous Italian had made his words seem even more extravagant. For the rest of his life, he would not be comfortable with English, the language his daughter would choose as her own, and he would never willingly speak it. He had tapped her chest through her coat, where her heart would beat. "You don't know yet how your roots will always call you home."

Shaking her head, Little stood up abruptly from where she sat, brushing at her eyes nonchalantly in case any tears dared stray down her cheek. She looked up to check for clouds, but there were none; it would be a hot day.

She was sure there was a café here somewhere, then remembered that in Italy they were called bars, which the Americans found confusing and funny; she would get herself a *cornetto* and cappuccino and bring Sira back a short espresso, dark with no sugar, the way she always took her coffee.

21

She patted her jeans surreptitiously and noted with relief that she had thought to shove a ten euro bill in her pocket before she had left the house. She turned her back firmly on Circus Maximus and the ruins that partly ringed it, ignoring the honking cars as she crossed the street and once again became a part of modern Rome.

***

After breakfast, Little was more malleable, and she headed back to the apartment. Humming softly, she noticed the vast number and funny outlines of the drinking fountains; waist-high oblong shapes with a rounded protrusion halfway up where the water gushed. They were locally referred to as the *nasoni*, literally translated as the big noses. The water caught the morning sunlight, turning it into rivulets of light. Even in the late spring heat, water was everywhere in Rome.

She found Sira in the hallway, carefully wrapping her signature scarf around her neck. This was always an ordeal, for Sira was very particular about her scarves. They were invariably silk, with varying patterns and colors—this one was alternating shades of green, from mint to moss to forest—and always folded into a half-diamond shape with the long part tucked into the back of her blouse in an effort to avoid the dreaded *colpo d'aria*.

Little perched herself quietly on a chair and watched as her aunt carefully knotted the silk scarf until it was just the way she wanted it, smooth and tucked neatly in the back, ruffled and carefully pressed to her neck in the front.

"It's diamond-bright outside," Sira began, reminding Little of another thing she had forgotten: the way her aunt described everyday things and made them seem shiny, important.

Little grinned. "Shall we go for a walk?"

"Absolutely! Are you going dressed like that?" Sira glanced over at Little's haphazard West Coast outfit of carefully ripped jeans, flip-flops, and a T-shirt.

"This is how I always dress…" Little ventured, considering for the first time that she might need to revise her wardrobe if she was to stay in this country.

"I know, but California and Rome aren't quite the same place." Sira scrunched her nose up and half-smiled, and Little knew she felt uncomfortable, too. In the past, Sira would have swatted at her and told her to go change. *Ah well, maybe feeling normal needs a little time to get caught up,* she thought to herself, changing into a less-ripped pair of jeans before offering her arm to her aunt. The two women walked out into the courtyard, heading for the bus stop.

***

They settled themselves onto the number 628 bus, the one that would bring them to the center, directly to Piazza Venezia. They could have simply walked over the Caelian Hill, Monte Celio, maybe wandered into the Villa Celimontana park; but the truth was that they needed public transportation, craved the bustle of strangers around them and the rumble of the machine underneath their feet, so that in the midst of it all they might grow comfortable with each other again.

The bus zipped past the church Sira sporadically attended, and she pointed it out to Little, who was starting to feel distinctly sleepy.

"See over there? That's where people can go to find spiritual solace during predetermined hours," she lowered her voice so that Little would know that gossip was coming. "I heard that after an attack on a woman one day in the empty church, the powers that be—not God, I don't think, but definitely as high up as the parish priest—locked the place down when nobody was around to supervise. I heard from the neighbor, you know the gossipy one who styles her hair into those terrible, bouncy ringlets? Well, she told me that the parish priest didn't like when the homeless used the church to sleep. I don't know which one of the stories is the truth, but I started noticing the way the priest speaks most kindly to the parishioners he thinks are more likely to be wealthy, myself included, and decided maybe going to church regularly isn't a huge necessity after all."

23

Little looked at her curiously. "I didn't realize you'd started going to church." Then she realized why her aunt might have been looking for solace and shut her mouth.

"Well, now I just pray silently, whenever I need to." Sira spoke clearly but quietly, for she never liked strangers to overhear her conversations. "I've decided there's no need for a middleman. If such an entity as God exists, then he can hear me talking to him just as clearly as he can hear that old priest yelling from his pulpit, maybe clearer." She finished by snapping her purse shut, her jaw set. Little couldn't help but smile; she knew that expression so well, had seen it so many times growing up when Sira had wanted to sound firm or determined, and now the familiar tone filled her with tenderness. She tentatively put one arm around her aunt's thin shoulders.

"I missed you, zia," she said, feeling her throat tighten.

"I know you did, Little. I missed you, too." Sira took Little's arm as they got off the bus and began to walk through the airy, crowded streets of the city center. A sudden gust of wind reached out and tore Sira's scarf from her neck, picking it up and twirling it above their heads, and as Little reached out for it the sun glinted through the greens of the silk and threw its colors across the two women. Little grabbed it from the sky and handed it back.

"The elements," said Sira, accepting it graciously, "are not in my favor today." They stopped for a moment while Sira folded the scarf, and Little helped her tuck the back into her blouse. When she was satisfied the spring wind would not have its way again, Sira took Little's arm once more and walked jauntily down toward the Via Margutta. Little vaguely remembered it as being known as the street of the artists, leading on to Piazza di Spagna. The piazza was so used to being flooded with people that on the rare occasion it was empty, it felt disconsolate. The breeze woke Little up slightly, and she tried not to think about how groggy she was starting to feel.

"Have you been to the house in Sperlonga lately?" Little asked, leading Sira over the cobblestones.

"Yes, I've gone with Anna a few times in the last months, since the weather got so nice early this year. Maybe soon we can head down for a few days."

"Sure," Little replied, although the idea did not remotely appeal to her. The last time she had been there had been with her father. The idea of going back now that he wasn't there made her feel as though she were trespassing on someone else's memories.

"We might have to sell it," Sira said, so softly that at first Little thought she had been speaking to herself.

"Oh?"

"Well, with my pension I can keep the apartment in Rome going, but the Sperlonga house is a bit of a stretch. Your dad," her breath caught slightly in her throat, "the money he left for it wasn't that much. The cancer treatments took a lot of his funds. The property taxes on the house alone take most of the money I set aside for maintenance."

Little felt her heart drop, not at the realization that there wasn't much money left, but because she had not known. Without so much as a whisper of complaint, Sira had handled everything. She now looked at Little as though Little might somehow blame her for having to sell her father's other home. The truth was that even though Little had been on scholarship at her university in San Francisco, her job was not providing the kind of income that would keep her in expensive California for much longer and the money she had put aside was rapidly running out. It had never occurred to her to ask for some of the money her father had left behind. Now, looking at the lines on the older woman's face, she was grateful that she had not. It gave her an odd sense of wrongness, somehow, that through no fault of her own Sira had borne the weight of it—the responsibilities, the cost, the emotional burden.

"If we have to sell, we sell. It's just a house," Little said as reassuringly as she could, feeling Sira's inquisitive gaze.

"Are you sure? I made promises to your father, Little. About taking care of you. When you first moved to California, and you were so small, and he asked me to make sure you stayed safe. I'm sure he thought there would be a point where he'd take over, but for me, when he passed, it was the same promise I made to him when you were a little girl."

"But you have! You have taken care of me, zia, but some things I just have to do for myself now. Listen. Any promises… they don't have anything to do with whether or not we own that house. We can do without the house."

Sira's face, however, indicated layers of concern that ran deeper than the future of a property. "There are some things I felt wrong about doing without you," she said carefully, slipping an arm through Little's, "like going through your father's things. Anna and I went through some of his files in Sperlonga, but we stopped. It didn't feel right without you there. It's one of the reasons I hoped you'd return."

"Of course. Right," Little said as bracingly as she could, even though the idea of going through her father's belongings made her stomach roll violently. She hoped vehemently that she wouldn't have to go through his things in front of Anna, with whom she hadn't felt comfortable for years. She did not want to have to watch as Anna lingered over every object, every room, and told its story, illustrating just how much she knew about Enrico's life that Little did not.

"Well, enough of that for now." Sira looked around at all the people bustling by on the famously luxurious shopping street of Via Condotti, the one that snaked out from Piazza di Spagna. The tourists were all pausing to look into the decadent windows of Valentino, Gucci, and Armani. "I don't know if you've kept up with what's going on in Italy at the moment, but I assume with what you study, you have." She glanced over at Little, who gave a nod of assent, still looking blankly at the passersby. "The brain drain, the rate of unemployment… I'm glad you're home, I can't deny that, but I'm not sure this is the best economy to throw you back into."

Little was remembering a conversation she'd had the week before. "Remember we were talking about Barbara? Her friend in Milan had applied to one of those employment agencies, and they called her in for an informational interview. She was really excited, and when she went they told her she had too much experience as a 28-year-old for Italian standards, so they couldn't give her one of the secretarial positions they would normally give someone her age, but that she was much too young for the higher-level positions. They suggested she start looking for work over in Switzerland."

Sira sighed. "I hear those things all the time."

They came out onto Piazza del Popolo and Little, realizing how far they'd walked and looking at Sira out of the corner of one eye to see if she was tired, spotted a bench and suggested they sit down for a while. Looking around at the vast piazza around them bordered by bustling shops, Sira asked Little what she had missed of Rome. For a moment, Little wanted to say that she had missed nothing at all, but the question seeped in and she could not help but consider it.

"I missed walking by the heavy oak doors of the old condominiums and hoping they might be open so I could sneak into the courtyards, which are so ethereal they seem like entrances to other worlds," she began, looking to the other end of the piazza, where a massive door stood locked against the people outside. These doors could lead to anywhere, from ministries to apartment complexes to private homes. Often the secretive entrances did not betray the nature of what was within, for Rome was a city that had adapted to modern times without losing its antiquity. Many times Little had walked by grandiose portals, imagining they must be the homes of royalty of some unknown nation, only to eventually discover the building within had been adapted to house rentable offices. This was why she liked to sneak into courtyards, to try to discern whom they belonged to, what they were.

"I missed going to see the Pentecost rose ceremony at the Pantheon," she continued. The thought of that square generated others, rich with scents and heat and tastes so alien to California. "I missed the warmth and the bustle, the markets and the fresh food, the whistling boys, and the lake at Villa Pamphilj, where there are so many turtles my friends and I call it Turtle Soup. I even missed the way Italian boys are so loud from far away but so shy at first approach. Do you remember that one winter weekend when the Colosseum was covered in snow? I ache for the awe of it…" She was smiling now and Sira was nodding, remembering how out of place it had seemed to see white enveloping the ancient structure. "I missed the way that everything here is human-sized, the tiny supermarkets, the one option of shampoo versus the endless varieties of cheese. I missed the way the Italians embrace the fact that they're made of skin and blood, bones and not iron. Humans who need a break from work between one and four every day, apparently. I missed *cornetti* in the morning and those two old ladies down the street that always have loud, intense arguments outside their apartments over how to make carbonara, their hands waving violently in the air. I missed how startlingly the monuments rise up in the middle of all this life, the cobblestone streets that turn into the Trastevere neighborhood, or Monti, the way you walk into a church and find yourself in front of a real Caravaggio."

What Little did not say, however, was that while it all sounded like a lot to miss, it still felt like she was talking about a place she went to visit sometimes, rather than a place to go home to.

"You know," Sira said, "I moved to California when I was quite young, when I got married. I can tell you that story another time, if you like. I gave birth to Anna there. That was my home, too. When my marriage fell apart, I came back to Rome." Sira seemed to have heard what Little had not said, and Little began listening more intently, curious about a part of her aunt's life that she had never known much about. Sira was looking ahead, one hand brushing back the short salt-and-pepper hair that tended to fall into her eyes when not carefully hair-sprayed into submission. "Then I decided to go back again. I missed the city I'd been married in, but then I knew I would also miss this city that had given me refuge when I felt that there was no corner of the world that I could use to escape the pain of a lost mate. Anna had grown close to my brother and chose to live her life here, in Italy. So, I was going back and forth between here and San Francisco, and because she was so safe and comfortable here I inadvertently left my child in my brother's care. Then, when you were born, Little, the circle closed itself. We didn't do it on purpose. We realized only years later that we had raised each other's children. A daughter for a daughter. A country for a country. Fair's fair." She shook her head lightly, as though trying to clear buzzing in her ears, and then got up. Little followed, wanting to hear more but not wanting to push her aunt. She had the distinct feeling Sira had been waiting to say these things to her, maybe waiting for the past two years, maybe longer.

They headed leisurely back to the bus stop with Little making sure that Sira kept to the paved part of the sidewalk, away from the cobblestones, so that she would not trip. It was her scanning of the side of the road that reminded her, strangely, of a scent.

"Aunty? Remember that cheese shop you and Dad used to take me to when I was little?" she asked suddenly, causing Sira to look up.

"Why, yes, of course," Sira answered. "You loved cheese, and so he used to stuff you with it. I couldn't stop him." She smiled, slowly, remembering. "So, you two would traipse off on your own, and I wasn't allowed to come. You must have been six, maybe seven. It was around here, wasn't it? Down one of these side streets…" Sira glanced down one of the many tiny roads that branched off from the main one. "That great family owned it. I can't remember their name, the Carli family? Yes, Carli. And they had those unbelievable cuts of prosciutto. I haven't thought about that place in years! They would take fresh *rosette*, and stuff them with *prosciutto cotto*, and…"

"And *provola affumicata*! That sharp cheese. I remember!" Little did remember, suddenly, and realized that was why she knew this road, and the smell of the shop. "That was some of the best cheese I've ever eaten. I can't believe I forgot!" she continued, thinking of the way Enrico used to take her hand and tell her gleefully to hold on to that hunger for just a while longer, that they would have the best sandwich in the world momentarily.

They continued walking down the street arm in arm, Little looking about interestedly for the shop that had popped up so brightly in her memory, as though it had always been there, waiting for her to come back to it.

"Zia?" Little began again, cautiously, reasoning that her aunt's upbeat mood was as good a reason as any to bring up uncomfortable subjects. "There are a couple of things that I was wondering about." She felt Sira's arm stiffen slightly, though her expression did not change. "I found a letter, back in San Francisco, among the things I had grabbed that used to be papà's." She pulled the folded piece of paper that she had carefully stowed in her pocket that morning and handed it to Sira, who took it slowly. "Do you know anything about this? It's typewritten, so I can't

29

figure anything out from the handwriting, although it mentions Delila, so I think Dad wrote it to her, but then why would he have it…"

Sira had stopped and was looking down at the page in front of her as though she could make it disappear simply by the intensity of her gaze. Then she flicked the page with one finger and handed it back to Little.

"No idea, Little. I'm sorry." She averted her gaze from Little's crestfallen expression.

"Really? But what about what he's saying?" Little thought she saw Sira flinch.

"I really don't know," she repeated. You know as much as I do about your mother. She wasn't much of one. There was that unfortunate incident when you were very young," Sira swallowed and looked at her niece, "and then you left to join me in the United States for a while to perfect your English and didn't want to return to Italy. From what I know, your mother eventually left. Your father didn't talk about it much. That's all I know." A small shrug.

"That's it? That's really it?" Little looked closely at her aunt, who as far as she knew had never kept anything from her before.

"That's what I know. The bus stop is just up here, I think I'll head back. Why don't you walk around a bit more?" Sira suggested. "I'm sure that shop is still around here somewhere. Put me on the bus home and have a wander." Little got the distinct impression that she was being gently dismissed.

"Yes, alright."

They were approaching the bus stop, and Little nodded as she saw the 628 heading down the street in their direction. She raised her arm to make sure it stopped, and helped her aunt climb on board.

***

As the bus pulled away, Sira gazed at her niece for a moment before settling into the hard plastic seat and proceeding to do one of the things she did best: sitting right in the middle of the chaos of a Roman springtime bus overloaded with people, and being entirely alone.

This skill had not come easily to Sira. When she had been younger, once in a while, she would be walking along, going over notes for a meeting or thinking of what to wear that evening, and all of a sudden she would look around, and the city and the people, the smells and noises and click-clack of shoes on the pavement, would smash into her. Panic would lap at her edges, and so she learned to close her eyes and find herself in a silent, shaded place just behind her eyelids. She had found a place of retreat that would always be there if she sought it out. It was so present, in fact, that she wondered if it had always been there, suspended, waiting for her to discover the refuge out of need.

In this place, there was only the smell of the sea and the tall ivory trees, the occasional melancholy star. She would build it in her mind just how she needed it just then, and it would come, more easily than anything else that she could touch in the physical world: sparkling cerulean lakes or deep hidden forests with twisting, curious vines; deserts made of colored sand that brushed against her face as she stood there, arms wide open, head tilted back to search out the sun, the moon, an eclipse. Sometimes there were shadows, and sometimes none at all, and sometimes there was nothing but an endless night sky and a vast room with vaulted ceilings and high, proud archways. There came a time when she didn't even have to close her eyes to conjure the images, and this was how she had found a way to breathe in the hardest moments of her life.

Watching the capital stream by outside the window, she let her mind cast back years and years, to a different Rome and a different bus, a different Sira. One who wanted to leave again, and was not sure how to go about it. The plane time options the travel company had given her sat patiently in her lap, and with her fingers playing solemnly over the edges of the wilting paper, Sira had considered the times and dates until they were just a series of numbers. She ran over the destinations in her mind, staring at the words "San Francisco" as though it were just another of many names on a sheet, with as much weight as any other place.

She had already known that she would miss Rome, because she had already left. She had known that she would miss the breezes typical of

31

this time of year, but also the sweaty summer days that made the cloth of her dresses stick damply to her body. She would miss the hum of the weekends spent in Verona, a city she prized almost as much as Rome itself. She would long for the Garden of Ninfa, the way it opened only a few months of the year, like a secret just outside of Rome, to reveal verdant gardens so otherworldly she thought heaven might turn out to be a lesser copy.

She would miss the Mediterranean, the warmer seawaters that caressed the coast of Sciacca, the town in Sicily where she went to escape the worst of the city heat, some years. She would miss the food in the south, the way it changed subtly but immediately as soon as she began moving up north, the way every place was bound by its food, the pride of its region. Looking out the window at the city—*her* city, the city of her family—at the colors thrumming past and the people complaining just behind her about the unfashionable heat, for a moment she had been horribly homesick for this place she had yet to leave.

The bus had heaved to a stop, and with a sigh, Sira had stood, wondering how it would feel to let the plane times fly out of her hands and into Piazza Venezia, taking their own flight over the Forum, breezing past the fountain named Trevi, spinning over the Barcaccia of the Berninis in Piazza di Spagna, swirling around the dome of Borromini's Church of Sant'Ivo, and then finally landing somewhere, anywhere but where she had been then. Her fingers had tightened around the paper.

And then, all those years later, she had finally decided to come back to Rome, to stop wandering. Right before Delila had found out the truth, before that horrible scene in front of Little, who was not much more than a baby then, at least in Sira's eyes. How she had made another promise to her brother, and taken Little away. She had warned him, hadn't she? That things broken had to be accepted as such. That you could build something new, without lies. Warned him not to deceive his daughter. And now, the past Little didn't know she had was threatening to make itself known.

With a start, Sira pulled herself out of her reverie and realized that the bus had almost reached her stop. She pressed the button the way

Little had shown her to when they had first come back to Italy together three years before, and with her head held high, as was her wont, she graciously stepped off the 628 and back into the chaos of her city, the things she remembered fanning out behind her in soft, slow patterns.

Chapter 5
Rome. Present day.

Little felt as though she had spent the entire afternoon walking down all of the tiny convoluted streets in the neighborhood in search of the Carli family shop. She tracked the steps she was sure she knew, hearing her father telling her younger self that the Carli family had been selling a variety of delicacies in that spot for as long as he could remember. He would tell her that one could trust them because everything they sold came from their little farm outside the city, deep in the countryside where, he said, they know the real meaning of what's fresh.

She knew she was in the right place. So why was this a toy store? While she sternly told herself not to be shy and to just go in and ask, a woman wandered to the open door of the store and peered at her. Little smiled tentatively.

"I'm sorry," she began, searching for a smile on the face of the woman who, she presumed, ran the shop. There was none. "I was looking for a sort of delicatessen?"

"Oh," said the woman, shaking mousy hair. "Da Carli. They closed down. I bought the place after them."

Little shook her head in response. "Are you sure? That can't be right. Why?"

The woman shrugged and picked up a stuffed giraffe that was sitting in the window, rearranging its spindly legs. "I don't know why. Never knew them. Just bought the place." She shook the bright yellow and orange giraffe vigorously, raising a cloud of dust.

"Alright. Well, thank you." Little felt she ought to say more, but the woman continued not to smile, so instead she tentatively raised a hand in salute. As the woman walked back into her store, closing the door behind her, Little turned on her heel to leave. *It's just a shop*, she told herself furiously, feeling tears rising unbidden. *Stop it. It's just a stupid shop.*

It wasn't long before all the streets began to look the same to her once again. She was growing more tired by the minute, and she wanted lunch. It was disconcerting how dirty many of the streets were, trash piled in heaps on the side of the road, smells she was not used to. Most surfaces were covered in graffiti; while some looked like art and added something to the street around them, most were angry scribbles, black marks cut into ancient buildings and landmarks.

She frowned and tried to remember if it had always been this way; she wasn't sure, but she didn't think so. Her father had always kept her in the parts of the city where beauty prevailed, and as she finally glimpsed a place she recognized—the Ostiense train station—she wondered if it wouldn't have been nicer to only know those places. *There is definite validity to the concept of ignorance being bliss*, she thought as she sidestepped a series of potholes in the sidewalk.

She walked aimlessly, mulling over her conversation with Sira. Little had never felt like she needed to know about her mother. Her life was full and she was loved from all sides: her aunt and father adored her, and she had had Anna, at least until the last few years; she didn't need anybody else. If she were being honest with herself, she had realized years before how a cold discomfort had entered the room whenever she thought to ask a question about her mother. She had felt guilty at what she was afraid would be perceived as a request for even more love than all that she had, when really, she was just curious. And there was the memory, the tiny one that made her crinkle her nose in discomfort. The cold slap, the feel of her mother's hand extended not in love but in violence. She and Sira had left for San Francisco soon after that, and she had never given it too much thought. But now, in addition to wondering why Sira would want to deflect her questions, she thought about the scrap of paper and the fragmented request it seemed to contain, and she wondered about the pieces of a story that she still did not know, but was nonetheless partly her own.

***

Little looked about as she walked. She was sure she remembered an underpass that connected the train station to the metro station. She pushed aside the question of Delila as she joined a crowd of people heading underground while she groped around in her bag for her headphones. These, she considered as she glanced about, were not tourists. These people were walking as though they were definitely Going Somewhere, a slight tension in their shoulders the only sign of discomfort in the dark surroundings. It wasn't until she had fitted both earbuds in her ears and flipped her iPod on that she realized the walkways on each side were lined with blankets.

Confused, she paused the song that had started playing and shifted to the left to get a better look. People were lying on the sides, sleeping on cardboard, wrapped in tattered blankets and seemingly oblivious to the sound of rushing footsteps a few feet away from their heads. Little stopped dead, entirely shocked mainly because nobody else seemed to be surprised, or even looking at all. She stood still until someone pushed her from behind, muttering as they shoved past her, and she was forced to keep walking.

As she followed the surge of people spilling out into the sunshine at the top of a set of stairs, Little looked at the humans around her, walking every which way, focused on wherever they were going, or whatever they were thinking. She wanted to reach out and tap them on the shoulder. Didn't you see them? But she was embarrassed, and so she looked in silence for the signs that would lead her to the metro.

The metro was packed, that lawless sort of crammed that she would have to add to the list of things she was not used to. For a few minutes she listened to the conversation of two women behind her, but when one complained to the other about how many people blocked the metros and trains for hours on end by being selfish enough to throw themselves in front of them, she phased out the conversation and focused in on the abundance of life all around her, packed into the tight space of the trembling metro walls. The machine itself seemed in dire straits in the high spring temperature, and Little thought how responsible it must feel for all the people on board, maybe for all the people out there. She sighed hard enough to ruffle the hair of the man standing in front of her, and as she raised a hand in apology she wondered if this was the life she had been running away from in Rome, the one where she was squooshed in the middle, people from all sides talking over her head.

Chapter 6
Sperlonga, Italy. Present day.

Little did not know how to express the anxiety filling her as they drew nearer to the house in Sperlonga. They drove down from Rome in the zippy new Fiat 500 they had rented that morning, and about half an hour outside of the city she decided it was best to say nothing at all.

"You drive stick shift very well," Sira ventured, not just to break the tension but because Little really did, even though she had always driven an automatic in the States. Little smiled tightly, but didn't say anything. She was thinking back to when she was fifteen, during a year that she had decided she would move back to Italy and make a life of it, as she had told all of her high school friends before what she had imagined was a grand departure. Of course, she had realized much too late, she had done it more for the announcement and the thrill of leaving than for the part where she actually left and went to live somewhere else. It had only taken a few weeks before she had panicked within the havoc of the capital, her homesickness rearing up.

Enrico, who had no idea how to deal with a teenage daughter he barely knew, still recognized in her something he had often felt himself—the claustrophobia of a big environment. Enrico loved bustle and company when he knew he also had the space to be alone, and he had built the house by the sea as a respite from the city. He'd brought Little there in the hopes that she would feel the same way.

Alone was all there was to be in Sperlonga in the shadow of winter, and Little had soon taken to dogging the paths that surrounded the house.

Straight out of the gate: turn right, she'd hit the sea; turn left, the forest. She had befriended the horses that rested in the paddock right outside the line of trees and had taken the dogs out for walks by the water that lasted miles, watching their paw prints padding along with her footprints. She had feared the point of the forest when she could no longer see the individual trees, and so had fostered the habit of walking straight into the shadows and turning, sitting in the moss, until the birds had eventually begun to treat her as though she belonged there, or at least as though she were not a threat, and therefore invisible. Out by the sea, there had been a rock jutting out just where the water began to deepen, and she had taken to repeatedly flinging herself off it, hitting the dark waves with a painful smack, drowning out the sound of the dogs barking madly on the shore. She would try to propel herself deeper, fighting the inevitable rise to the surface, knowing that when she opened her eyes she would always see colors. She had forced herself to face every fear, except the one of learning who her father was.

She had been certain she had known, really. Didn't she know everything, after all? She knew she resembled him, that they had the same shade of dark eyes, that they even walked the same way, back straight, with determined footsteps. She recognized his tendency to draw within when feeling threatened or uncomfortable. When backed into a corner, he did exactly what she did: flung himself out the door and took to the wintry beach for walks that could last miles. They could each see flashes of themselves in the eyes of the other, but did not know how to reach out and touch those pieces.

In the best of times, Little delighted in fancying herself a hybrid, a wanderer; when she felt lost, she simply felt ill put together, a forgotten charge. She had begun to wake with a start in the middle of the night, haunting the hallways she had been a child in, trying to force herself to feel at home again.

She would pace into the living room, where in her mind the lights would flicker on to a warm, hazy gaze and the whole family would be there again, sitting at the big table in the center of the room, the one that could be extended to fit more people. Enrico would sit in the middle, eyes sparkling, and Little would feel so proud to be his daughter. He had been a jovial man when surrounded by those he loved.

Anna and Little, who was not yet a teenager, would sit next to each other and laugh at each other's inside jokes, an army of two. Though there was a significant age difference between them, Anna had always known all of Little's secrets. She had been the first one Little would run to during any family skirmish, or when she had needed advice about boys, or nail polish, or how to calm Sira down when she caught you doing something you had promised you wouldn't do. Anna, having grown up before Little in the same family, had always seemed to understand her, to be a staunch ally. When had that changed?

During that winter, padding quietly in the dark, the gentle, huge family dogs as her shadow, Little would sometimes come upon her father in his bedroom and find him sitting on the edge of the bed in the dark, facing the window that he always kept flung open, his head in his hands. She had never gone in. What else did she need to know?

Whenever she opened the big front door to the garden, the dogs would come running. Enrico had called them guard dogs, but when it was cold outside he'd let them in to sleep by the fire. *They can guard when it's warmer*, Enrico would say, *they have bad backs*. He used to tell her that they looked just like Brenno, the dog he'd had years before Little was born. Brenno was a dog of lore for Little, who heard of him from both Enrico and from Sira, who had also loved him dearly. Sira would begin by putting a hand up past her hips and say that he'd been more than half her size, that she was certain that he'd been part wolf, and that her brother's story that he picked him up from a breeder somewhere on the outskirts of Rome had always been a lie. Enrico had admitted years later that he'd gotten him from a farmer near the Val d'Aosta, letting his little niece Anna pick out the runt of the litter. The farm had bumped up against wildlands, and when Enrico had asked the farmer who the father of the little runt was, the man had only grunted and nodded in the direction of the forest. Enrico, looking the pup in his yellow eyes, had asked no more questions. They'd always been a shepherd family, but not pureblood by rule. Enrico liked the underdogs, as did Little, and there were many occasions when they felt more comfortable around their animals than they did around most people.

The house had been cold then. It was hard to heat a house that big, meant for a big family, especially when there were only two people there. Enrico had clearly had it built in preparation for their family expanding, growing closer, coming here for the summers and the holidays where he would be patriarch. At that time, Little had never thought to wonder what it must have felt like to have a broken family, with a sister and a daughter that lived on the other side of the world, on what must have felt like another planet.

In her last month there, he had insisted on taking her out to learn to drive stick shift. He would huddle against the side of the car and turn the heat on, and it was only much later that Little realized that he was already sick then, that her father, who had always eschewed heating because he radiated warmth like a furnace, had started feeling cold all the time. When she would look at him curiously, he'd smirk at her, shoulders straightening.

"You don't start the car in third, Little. Come on, try again." He was trying desperately to make up for lost time, though that was another thing she hadn't realized then, make up for the things he had never been able to teach her because she had chosen another place over him, and because he had chosen to let her. It wasn't until after he had died, when somebody asked her where she had learned to drive stick shift so well and she had responded proudly that she had learned from her father, that it had hit her like a train. He had done it for that moment, for when she would say, *my father taught me how to do that.* Unable to connect with her in the right now, he had been marking himself in her future. Because he had realized he was running out of time with her.

She had not known then, still did not know now, about the books he had liked to read, or his favorite colors. She didn't know about the women he had loved, or if he was grateful to Sira for raising her, or jealous, or that mixed-up something that lies between decided emotions. She did not know if shaving made him itch, if thunder made him feel afraid or free, if he liked it when it was foggy or bright outside. She also absolutely had not known that when he felt lost or confused or afraid, he had taken to writing stories.

In those cold days in a lonely house where she had begun to feel more like a memory of herself than the incarnate version, Little had taken to washing her hair and leaving it hanging down her back to air-dry. She had stopped caring how it looked. While she had read, hunched over, Enrico would put two fingers on the top of her spine and say, "You'll have arthritis when you're older if you don't dry that hair." She would roll her eyes.

"Pretty sure that's an old wives' tale, Dad."

Until finally one day, when they had both been sitting in the washed-out living room, he had pulled out the ancient hairdryer and told her to sit down. She had opened her mouth to tell him that there was no way, absolutely no way, that she was going to let him dry her hair, because she was an adult. But when she had met his eyes, a reflection of her own, she had closed her mouth again and sat down with a thump. She had let him get on with it, the sound of the hairdryer humming along happily. His fingers had been infinitely gentle, and he had never tugged a knot without working it out first so that he would not hurt her.

Sometimes, now, Little wondered what would have happened if she had stayed then; if she hadn't left him and Italy a few months later, alienated and hungry to go back to what was familiar, telling herself and everyone else that it was because she didn't want her grades to suffer during such important years of her schooling. If she had not been so eager to once again take on the relationship with Enrico that she had grown accustomed to, the one where he was a telephone father, a vacation father. If she had stayed, would she have noticed that he never seemed to be able to get warm? Would she have recognized that the cold that he developed, the one that never went away, was a symptom of something far more dangerous? Could she have warned him?

"Little?" Sira's voice broke through Little's memories, and Little realized her hands were gripping the steering wheel so tightly that her knuckles had gone white, that she had been driving without thinking.

"Yes?"

"We're here." Ah. So they were. A dark green Fiat Punto was already neatly parked outside the front gate.

43

"Is that Anna's car?"

"It is."

"Awful color."

Little bit her tongue, not wanting to say anything else unpleasant. She felt increasingly uncomfortable as Sira unlocked the gate to the white-walled house surrounded by a neat garden. It gave the impression of being the coziest, most snug place in the world. If she could be honest with herself, what she wanted was for everything to go back to the way that it had been, back when Sperlonga only meant sunny beach days and languid summer meals spiced with *prosciutto e melone* on the front deck, when it didn't come complete with estranged cousins, angst over her father, and the clenching fear of having to sell his house. *Assuming it would sell*, she realized, remembering all the For Sale signs they had passed on their way here. People weren't keeping their traditional second homes anymore.

Anna opened the door for them, soberly dressed and with a matching expression on her face. She reached out automatically to help her mother in the front door and largely ignored Little's presence, which suited Little down to the ground. Sira's only daughter, Anna had her father's light hair and eyes as well as his temper, though she also resembled Little in her manner, a fact which Sira observed and the other two stoutly ignored. There is something about deeply loving the same people that makes you similar; this is how Little and Anna mirrored each other, although they tried not to notice.

Little had not realized at what point they had begun to grow apart—if there had been a precise moment when Anna's expression was no longer laughing when she looked at Little—but when Enrico had died, a bitter fight had exploded between them. Ostensibly, it was because Anna had heard that Little wasn't going to stay in Italy, but it really seemed to be about something else that Little didn't quite understand. Anna had felt wronged by Little's waywardness, whereas Little had felt betrayed by someone she had both loved and admired, and they simultaneously nursed those hurts with care.

The three of them went from room to room, picking up bits and pieces, opening the windows, all avoiding Enrico's old bedroom in the back of the house. His room was the one that let the most light in. The house was simply arrayed, with every room incorporating the deep wooden paneling that Enrico had found both elegant and comforting, as well as small, brightly painted knickknacks from his travels adorning the shelves. Her father had been a collector of fine, delicate objects, priding himself in rooting out little symbols that made his space charming, full of memories of the places he'd traveled. *I like things to remind me*, he'd say, picking up a peculiarly shaded pebble, *without screaming their name at me*.

In the main living room, just in front of the fireplace, stood a veritable tower of cardboard boxes.

"These were brought up from Enrico's studio in the garage," Sira explained, moving to open the first box. Anna set it on the sturdy wooden table that dominated the center of the large room, where it would be easier for Sira to go through the contents. Then she took hold of another of the boxes, set it on the table next to her mother, and began methodically removing the tape that kept it closed.

"No wonder you're a surgeon, Anna. That looks like it's going to take you about half an hour. I don't think you're going to hurt it if you just rip it off, yeah? Or did you want to inject a squirt of anesthesia in case it starts screaming and hops off the table?" Little grabbed the box next to her cousin's and hauled it onto the floor. She looked up in time to see Anna's eyebrows disappearing into her hairline but could have sworn she caught Sira stifling a grin.

"Oh sorry, Little, I prefer to do things properly and do as little damage as possible, unlike some people I could name, who prefer to destroy everything in sight while trying to figure out how to open an envelope."

"Apologies, I can't hear you over the sounds of cardboard box disembowelment. You may want to scoot to avoid ink sprays. Should you even be opening boxes? Don't you risk your professional surgeon's hands?"

"Oh, that's hilarious Little, is that what you've been learning over in California, the complicated art of being even more difficult?" Anna stopped abruptly at Sira's sudden coughing fit.

"Anna, speaking of your being a surgeon, I've been meaning to ask you how your practice is going." Sira smoothed a wayward hair out of

45

her eye and barely glanced at Little, who got the hint and focused once again on the contents of her box. It seemed filled with the same sort of decorations that littered the rooms of the house—small clay figures, tiny delicate boats, the occasional seashell. She glanced at the mementos for a moment longer before pushing them aside to pull out the stacks of paper on the bottom. She began, carefully, to go through the pages, notebooks with phone numbers scribbled across the front next to reminders that Enrico had written to himself, tiny passages. Anna and Sira's conversation was a comforting buzz behind her, and she soon grew so engrossed in the tiny intricacies of the hasty notes and brochures her father had kept that she barely noticed when, drawing out more papers from the box, a small figurine fell from her hands and crashed onto the floor.

"Hey!" she heard Anna call, and watched, surprised, as Anna snatched the little figure off the floor and cradled it in her hands. It was a hand-sized decorative Pinocchio doll wearing a jaunty green hat, and Little remembered that it had hung in the window of the garage. Anna picked up the little wooden foot that had cracked off in the fall and glared at Little.

"Relax, Anna, it isn't anything important," Little said, feeling even more out of place.

"These are his things, and they're precious," Anna retorted, nodding at the piles of paper and notebooks that Little had stacked neatly beside the box. "Those things are important to you. Well, these things are important to me." She turned away and walked out of the room, holding the little doll-like figure in one hand. Little, completely nonplussed, looked at Sira, who looked equally baffled as she got up and followed her daughter out of the room.

***

Little was sitting on a tree stump in the back garden, watching the last of the light fade through the lemon trees, when she heard Sira pull up a chair next to her. She glanced over and smiled.

"Is Anna alright?" she asked.

"She's upset," Sira admitted.

"About a toy?"

"About a toy. I've thought many times that some of life's worst pains stem from the rearranging of detritus after the end, whatever that end is. We're cleaning up. It's going to be hard," Sira said. Little shifted her shoulders slightly; she felt as though a great, immense weight were attempting to place itself squarely upon her. She tried to dislodge it.

"This was your father's dream house," Sira continued, looking about as the breeze gently shook out the trees that surrounded them, the leaves playing the gentlest of bells. "He built it to be peaceful. I never thought we'd have to sell it."

I never thought he would die, Little almost said, but didn't.

"So we're going to sell this house?" Sira said, and it sounded like a question.

"Yes," Little acknowledged.

"To be lighter."

"Alright."

"To start again. We'll call an agency, then. To discuss putting it up for sale." Something slid into place in the back of Sira's eyes, and from the glint, it looked like steel. She stood up and patted Little lightly on the knee. "Come on then, Little. Let's get back inside, rummage around a bit more, have something to eat. No point sitting out here, avoiding Anna."

***

Anna and Little mostly ignored each other as they waded through the remainder of the boxes, and Little tried not to roll her eyes when she saw the little wooden Pinocchio propped up against a picture frame on the coffee table. She felt like she should apologize, but though she kept opening her mouth to do so, no words presented themselves. She pressed her lips together and kept sorting until she got bored enough to start poking about the shelves in the living room. Perusing through a small side drawer, her fingers nudged something smooth, with rounded edges. She slid it out from under the piles, and held what looked like a small plastic bracelet up to the light.

"What is this?" she asked. Sira wandered over and peered at it, lips turning into a questioning expression. "I've never seen it before," Little continued, reading the minuscule writing inked on the paper tucked into the plastic. "It has my name on it. I don't recognize the handwriting." Anna glanced over and then returned to her own investigation of the papers sitting on the mantle over the fireplace. Sira gently took the bracelet from Little's outstretched hands so that she could look at it up close.

"Why, that's the date you were born, and the time, 2:05 p.m.," Sira said. "Boy, do I remember... your dad was so excited he kept jumping around the waiting room, telling me his daughter was being born." Sira laughed, her eyes far away. "It looks like... "

"It's the bracelet they put on newborn babies," Anna cut in, dusting her knees off as she stood up and turned to face the other two women in the room. Little looked at her curiously.

"With their details. *Zio* Enrico kept yours." Anna shrugged at Little's frown.

"How did you know that, dear?" Sira asked, looking questioningly at her daughter.

"He told me at some point, I think, and then I saw it here, after he died. Left it in the same place." Anna was shifting her weight from foot to foot, not quite meeting Little's eye.

"How come you didn't tell me?" Little found her voice, taking the bracelet back from her aunt.

"Figured you would find it eventually, if you ever came back. And then I forgot about it. And you weren't here to tell anyway, were you?" Anna replied, finally raising her eyes to meet her cousin's.

Little suddenly felt the tension of the last days, coiled within her, hardening into hurt anger. She glared at Anna hotly, realizing even as her temper flared that she probably wasn't being very fair, which only made her angrier. Anna regarded her coolly, although color was rising in her cheeks.

"Why didn't you just tell me?" Little repeated, not quite keeping the wobble out of her voice, although she was trying hard. Anna raised her eyebrows and shrugged.

"I didn't think it was *important*." There was a faint suggestion of a smile in Anna's reply, and Sira sighed. Little looked around, at the spacious wood-paneled room that they were standing in. Her father's possessions were strewn everywhere, little pieces bobbing in an unfamiliar place that belonged to someone else, that she only just recognized, and even then, from far away.

"I already feel like I didn't know him," Little started trying to explain, to relieve the pressure in her chest. "Maybe this," she held up the little object in her hand, "would have helped."

"Would it have?" Anna said, all color bleached out of her face. "And this is about you again, is it? How Little feels in this house, how hard it was for Little to lose her father." Anna's fists clenched involuntarily as she visibly tried not to show her anger. "How Little gets to mope about since she did us all this big favor in coming back, which cancels out that she had left everybody behind."

Anna's voice caught, and Little opened her mouth to answer, but Sira shook her head, almost invisibly, and Little stopped. Anna took a deep breath and paused, seeming uncertain for a moment, then seemed to decide to go ahead.

"How long are you going to stick it out this time before you scuttle off again anyway, huh? You felt like you didn't know him because you *didn't* know him. *I* knew him. He raised *me*."

Everything was still, and suddenly Little felt as though she were fighting someone else's ghosts, or walking through something sticky and slow, like molasses. It sounded like the same fight they'd had when Little had left.

In the silence, Sira pulled a chair away from the heavy oak table in the middle of the room and sat down.

"Girls, do you not think it's time to talk?" She had never been good at initiating conversations like this; when faced with emotions that shook control, she tended toward reticence. "Sit down," she tried.

The two did, on either side of the monarch of their family. Sira sighed, made a movement as though to rest her hand on Little's, still tightly curled around her baby bracelet, and then let it drop.

"There has been enough pain, I think. The fact is, sometimes you just have to say things as they are." Sira spoke slowly, enunciating carefully. "I don't know what the issue is between you two, except that I worry all the lines got crossed; who raised who, who loved who more, who belongs where. And when Enrico died," Sira dropped her head, "when my brother died, the glue dissolved."

Anna and Little pointedly did not look at each other.

"I know that I can't expect these wounds to heal right now," Sira continued, "but I thought it was worth it to put it out there, where it can all air out." She looked at the other two, who were facing away, one toward the window, one looking at the far wall, toward the door.

Sira was surprised and saddened by the silence; her girls had always been vocal. Though they all spoke a mix of English and Italian to each other, heated moments brought out their arterial languages. When Sira became angry, she inadvertently slid into an even quieter Italian, syllables peaked in ice. Little simmered into English, her words biting, and to her consternation, she had difficulty controlling the level of her voice. Anna also tended to raise her voice, though her language of choice was Italian. All through their separate childhood years, both had experienced that moment when Sira would drop the point of an argument to look at them imperiously and say, "You don't have to yell, you're not at a fish market." Both now fully grown, Little and Anna still rolled their eyes whenever they smelled fish, at a market or otherwise.

"I was thinking while you were gone, Little, and maybe you don't know enough, about this country, about our family."

"Because she never *cared to know*," threw in Anna, but a warning glance from Sira closed her mouth again.

"Maybe that's not fair, either," Sira continued, "to expect you to feel allegiance to a group of people that you never got to know. I can try to tell you some things, if you like." This time there was a flicker of reaction from both Anna and Little.

"Maybe we should have some dinner first," Anna suggested, which Little surmised was the Italian way of saying fighting can wait. Between the three of them, it was decided that a quick plate of carbonara might do nicely, and they set about pulling together a meal.

50

***

"Let me tell you a story, girls. Anna, you know a lot of this, but maybe not all of it, and I don't think you've ever heard it from me."

The pasta had done much to calm the tension in the room, as is the tendency with carbohydrates, and the three women were once again seated around the table, less hungry and more relaxed. Tense as Anna and Little were around each other, neither one was about to give up a good story from Sira.

"Let me color in the background, fill in the surroundings. Tell you, just quickly, what happened before. Sometimes I feel like you two are walking around in the dark, fighting battles with each other about a family you've only caught the tail end of. Life is like a game of chess, no? You like checkers better? You're right, they're simpler. Still, though, two opposing sides. Here's the secret—that's why these games aren't like real life at all. The truth is, you'll wish it were that simple. The nuances of millions of colors are enjoyable only when they highlight your life. When you stumble along the grays and browns of confusion, stillness, uncertainty... Well. It takes all sorts. Still, though, I have to tell you about how the pieces were set up, so that you can understand why they fell the way they did...

"The war was what it was," she continued. "You've heard war stories before. I'll tell you what I know, bit by bit. But first, can I tell you about your grandparents? On your father's side, of course. They are the building blocks, after all. You young ones, I wish you knew yourselves enough to understand what these building blocks tell you of yourselves, how you are brand new but also little bits of not brand new.

"Sometimes, when you're caught by surprise—and don't look away, Anna, I'm speaking to you, too—you start and then, immediately, hunch your shoulders. As if you were preparing for something. You've both done it since you were little. I never have. Anna, I know you knew your grandfather well, but Little never met him. He always used to do it. I know lots of people do some variation of this. But something in your expression. It's the same, as if you were imitating him. So how come that happens? Why do we pick up tendencies from people who are in our blood but never in our lives? Ack, don't tell me about engrained habits and passed-down psychological traits. Science doesn't explain everything. Oh, lots, sure. But not everything. Not by a long shot. You learn that down the line, too.

"It's a shame you never met your *nonno*, Little. He was a great man. I'm not just saying that. I've met a lot of men. Trust me on this, there are not a lot of great ones, so don't go throwing the term around as soon as you meet someone you like. Being great is something you only know after a long time, after you see someone in their deepest, darkest places and in their most cherished hour. There is a reason for light and dark. They reflect different things. See them when the days are long and monotonous, short and angry, languid and dreamy. When they're being pushed to the limits, when they are adored and also scorned. Then you can tell me someone is great. Your grandfather was great. Of course, I am his daughter, and I know that you think time has colored my thoughts, or that, like most daughters, I'm convinced my daddy could do no wrong. But I've never made saints out of people unless they deserved it. My memories are crystal clear. I'll never remember anybody like I remember him. Do you have anybody like that? Where every movement, every glance, automatically etches itself into your being? As if your brain knows right away, this is going to be important. No, don't tell me. Some things shouldn't be the consequence of a question.

"My life started in another age. Some people reach my age and say they feel nothing but tired. I'm tired, too, you know. But I'm a hell of a lot more curious than I am tired. I do wonder if other near centuries have moved quite so quickly. The things that have happened in my lifetime, I would not have dreamed of in the beginning. I *am* rather proud of that, you know. The first time you showed me the little video on your computer with the talking people, I wanted to run screaming from the room. And now I know how to use it! Not bad, right? Yes, I know it's called Skype. What do you mean, it's not pronounced skai-pey?

"Families were different then—having many children was the norm. Your grandfather was one of nine children. How many people do you know that have that many children now? Or that have more than one?

Or any, even? All of the brothers went to the Great War. Two of them never came back. Your great-grandmother used to knit socks, thinking your great-grandfather could drop them off 'at the war.' She had no idea that you couldn't just walk there, that people would go anywhere that they could not reach on foot. Nobody had the heart to tell her. She knit socks for years, warm socks for the feet of the sons that she could not protect. Is that sad? Or is that not sad? Your nonno looked for his lost brothers for the rest of his life. That was what he was like. He used to go up to Trieste to look for their graves, even when I was little, and so much time had passed by then. I used to imagine him—tall, broad-shouldered, green-eyed, searching through rows of headstones. He never found them, of course.

"He died too young, my father. He got through two wars, ushered his children through one, and I suppose his heart had had just about enough. I dreamt it. I was following him into church, the same one we walk by often, girls, the beautiful one on Via Gallia in Rome. He would always hold my hand on the way in. I hated church. It was dreary and boring, and even more than seventy years on I can tell you I've rarely met a priest or a nun I get along with. But I loved it when we got to go with him, because afterward he'd take all three of us children to get those chocolate squares and the fresh rosette, that bread that's baked in the shape of a rose. Only on Sundays, because they didn't make that chocolate on any other day. He used to tell us it was a secret and not to tell mother, but of course now I realize that they must have been in on it together. But oh, back then it was such a delicious secret to us! We'd wipe the chocolate off each other's mouths so nothing would give us away, and we could taste it the whole walk home. They used to wrap the chocolate in red paper. I've always loved red paper. They don't make chocolate or bread like that anymore, and don't you roll your eyes at me because it's true.

"In my dream, he wouldn't let me go into church with him. It was just me and him outside the church, and I kept trying to take his hand but he shook me off, would not talk to me, turned his face away. I was so mad! He turned, finally, and looked at me the way he always used to when he wanted me to know that he was being serious, scrunching down so that we were almost eye to eye. He put his hand on my shoulder, shaking his head. I understood. Stay. So I stayed. I would have never gone against your grandfather when he gave a direct order. He so rarely gave them. He never had to. We all wanted to please him.

"Then he stood up, the tallest man in the world, and strode into the church with his shoulders back. I heard him shut the door firmly, urgently, behind him, as though worried I would try to follow him in. He was making sure that I was going to stay out. When I woke up I remembered that he was wearing a beautiful suit, handsomely cut, and that he looked so majestic. I had never seen that suit before, and I wondered where I had imagined it from. I tried to shake the dream from my mind, did not speak of it to anyone.

"When he had the heart attack two weeks later," Sira ended quietly, "my mother bought him that suit to bury him in."

The fire had died down, but no one had made a move to bring it back to life. Little and Anna both sat in their chairs, backs straight, leaning forward and not daring to move. Little glanced over at Anna and remembered, with a start, that when Sira said the word grandfather, she meant grandfather to both of them, that the places they came from were parallel. Another thought ran through her mind: If Anna resented Little for the life that she had lived, then the same logic would give Little the right to resent her older cousin for the family that she had known, the family that Little hadn't had the chance to know.

But she didn't want to start reasoning that way.

Sira looked up. "At your father's funeral, Little," and then, looking at Anna and knowing her daughter would feel gratified, "I know in a lot of ways, it was your father's funeral as well. That was why I stopped outside the church. Why I didn't want to go in. I know it upset you both, and I am sorry. But I thought of my father, in his beautiful suit, and of never seeing him again after that, not ever again. I couldn't bear it. I couldn't bear to watch you both lose him. I couldn't bear to lose my brother, too."

54

***

When the sun rose the next morning, it found the three women in separate parts of the house. Anna stood at the window of her bedroom, the one that faced the sea. Sira, waiting for the coffee to finish brewing, opened the kitchen window so that she could see the light trickle into the day. Once again, Little was walking through the hallways that led to the large, wooden back door, trying to remember what it felt like when Enrico's presence filled all of the rooms, and thinking that this was the difference between then and now. It wasn't necessarily that it was simpler then, she reasoned; it was just that this was his home, and when he had been here, it had been complete. He had left it behind, but that didn't make it not his anymore, at least not as far as the walls and the garden were concerned. Maybe, Little considered sadly, her own presence was not strong enough to fill a home. She was also still thinking about what her aunt had said to her and Anna last night. It had made her think and want to ask about that feeling she had had in her apartment in San Francisco, looking at the television screen as something that could have been a memory marched by. She was almost sure that her aunt had avoided that conversation, too, the way she had avoided talking about the note the other day in Rome. She had almost asked about her father and Delila, but she had not wanted to ask about either of those things in front of Anna. As if on cue, she looked up to see Anna leaving her room and heading to the kitchen, noticing Little but not acknowledging her. Little sighed and headed for the kitchen herself, thinking of what Sira had told her about picking up the pieces, cleaning up after someone's life.

***

"Oh, Little. Here," said Anna, handing her a small sheaf of papers as they were filing out a few hours later. They were nowhere near finished with going through Enrico's belongings, but the job would be long and they had decided that it would have to be done in increments. Little reached out for the paper and stiffened, recognizing the handwriting. She looked back up at Anna; they might not get along, but Anna had rarely been gratuitously mean in regard to Little's father, whose memory drew them close together and, on principle, kept them apart.

Anna handed the page over, taking her car keys out of her purse with the other hand.

"I found it downstairs in the garage. It was on the desk; it must have gotten left there. I know you're into this writing stuff. Might be worth it to have a look down there in general; I didn't have a chance to go through the rest of his papers downstairs there. And the house in Rome, too."

Little took the yellowed paper slowly out of Anna's hands, running her fingers lightly over her father's firm writing of the word Starlings. Was he really gone? Was he really gone if she could still feel the indentation of his handwriting? Little realized her hand was trembling as she skimmed the story; before getting into the driver's seat, she opened the back door and laid the bundle down gently in the middle seat to avoid it becoming any more creased. If Sira thought this strange, she didn't say anything. As Little eased the car into the thick Rome-bound traffic, thoughts whirled through her brain. *When did you feel like this, papà? When did you write this? And why didn't I know?*

Starlings

The boy goes flying down the stairs, turns the corner out onto the street at breakneck speed. He can imagine his mother screaming at him, *"Ti romperai l'osso del collo!" You'll break your neck!* He's grateful that she can't see him, not this moment when she's tucked upstairs in the kitchen making dinner before his father gets home. She's making him pasta alla gricia, which his papà loves because of the abundance of the sharp *pecorino romano* cheese, even though *mamma* says it makes him fat and if his heart gives out before he's sixty then she'll have told him so, won't she, but she'll make it anyway because there has been less and less work and he comes home with darker eyes every day. She'll make him *gricia* in the hope that he'll tease her about it like he used to, back before every conversation was about whether or not they'd be able to make ends meet this year, but he won't, and the boy, Giacomo, will lower his eyes to his plate and pretend he doesn't know why she made the meal in the first place. He'll pretend she made it for him.

He rips onto Via Urbana and he can smell his neighborhood, Monti, immediately. Mamma says she used to be able to recognize everyone on these streets, but she can't anymore, not anymore, she grumbles. But his neighborhood is still his neighborhood, and every other face is one that has watched him grow up, every other face is a friend (and maybe the rest are future friends), and those aren't bad odds after all, are they? The *fruttivendolo* on the corner yells out, *"Giacomino, ma dove corri?" Giacomino where are you running to?* And without missing a beat the boy answers, *"Sto andando via per sempre!*' laughing, *I'm going away forever!* That was his favorite line, until one day mamma whipped around and yelled at him to stop saying it, stop it, stop it. Now he never says it in front of her anymore, because he might get a slap, but sometimes, when it's like this, running through his Roman neighborhood, his neighborhood, his place in the world, free and indigenous, he loves to scream it out to the wind, imagine the words bouncing off the shimmering terra-cotta walls. Forever, forever!

Monti is his. He has always known this, and it is a powerful truth for a little boy to have. It isn't dusk quite yet, and this city, this city owns this in-between time, this nowhere-everywhere time. The open shop doors throw long lights onto the intervening shadows, and Giacomo leaps, bounds so that he never has to touch the dark spots. They seem like bad luck, and there is so much light that it doesn't take much to avoid the elongated darkness creeping, creeping into night.

Monti is glittering at this hour, and if it weren't for the Christmas lights twinkling above him (even though it's January), he could be running through the streets three hundred years ago. He finally hits Via Cavour, eyes automatically scouting for his destination: the *merceria*, the neighborhood shop filled with a million things any household needs. There's one in every neighborhood, seemingly always owned by an elderly couple or lady who will tell whoever will listen about her family running this business for generations. With nimble fingers, she will individually wrap whatever it is mamma has sent him in here to pick up—undershirts, ties, a gift for the neighbor, and, once, yards of blue silk ribbon for his sister's birthday.

He looks for the old door with the beautiful sign above it, sure the shop will still be open; *la signora* Luisa won't close before seven in the evening, and it's not even six yet! She'll look him up and down, imperiously, and without a word he'll know she finds him lacking. Giacomo is sure this is why her husband always slips him a sweet on his way out. He wonders who gives her husband a chocolate for putting up with signora Luisa, but he never says that out loud.

Luisa has run this shop her entire life, like her mother before her, everything in its beautiful neat rows, encased in the dark brown wood shelves that her father had built with his own strong, knowledgeable hands. Luisa knows where everything is without having to look, almost before she is asked for it. Sometimes Giacomo wonders if she can read his mind, and hopes not, because Luisa's daughter is about his own age and he's just waiting to turn ten so he can ask her for an *aperitivo*. Luisa would kill him if she knew that. He's not certain what aperitivo is yet, but it seems all the rage with the teenagers he tries to hang around, and anyway, he has plenty of time to work out the details.

By now he has walked up and down the street several times and knows he can't have missed the door, not when he is nine and has been running errands here since he was old enough to walk and not waddle. Brow furrowed, he spots an empty space above a padlocked door. He has never seen the door barred, and glances around to make sure he is on the right street. But yes, right next to it is the *fioraio*, the flower shop. He walks right up to the entrance, resting his warm hands against the cool glass, trying to look into the dark interior. At first, it looks empty, but he recognizes the counter, and with a sinking heart, the empty shelves behind it.

"*Ha chiuso*," the gravelly voice says, and he whips around. It's the flower vendor, a middle-aged woman. *They have closed.*

"*Come? Ma perchè?*"

"*Per fallimento. Si vergognavano a dirlo, hanno chiuso così, di botto.*" *They went bankrupt. They were ashamed to say it, they closed, suddenly.* She shakes her head, looks back up at the sign to her store. "*Forse presto succederà anche a me. Non so che cosa ti serviva, ma c'è un centro qui vicino. Hanno tutto. Meno che la personalità.*"

Her words sink in: *Maybe soon it will happen to me as well. I don't know what you needed, but there's a shopping center nearby. They have everything. Except the personality.*

Giacomo doesn't remember what he needed, and for some reason a cold knot has started to form in his stomach. He doesn't want to go home and tell his father that the store has closed. He remembers his father telling him that he's been buying his ties there since he was old enough to wear them.

On the walk home, the little boy drags his feet. He raises his eyes only when he sees the massive formation of starlings, the *storni*, etching figures into the sky, the migration typical of this time of year. They always fascinate him, these little birds, flying mightily in formation, capable of something so beautiful as a dance in the sky, yet if he saw one alone he would never imagine what it could do with those little wings.

And he remembers when he asked his mamma why she was so mad at him for saying that he will go away forever. She had bent her knees so that their eyes had met, looked straight at her son.

"*Perché è la verità.*"

Because it is the truth.

Chapter 7
Rome. 1970.

The summer during which Sira came to Italy to spend some time with her brother and her daughter had been a particularly hot one. Enrico was staying at the house in Narni during those hot, humid months; he had taken little Anna with him, since, as she loved to remind anybody and everybody who would listen, she was on holiday break from school.

Tucked on the top of a small mountain nearby (a hilly incline, Sira was inclined to call it, so little did it resemble a mountain) was a tiny abbey, so rustic that it had no running water. Sira knew that Enrico enjoyed taking Anna with him when he went to the well to fill up barrels with water and drive them up to the priests on his little jeep, skirting the canyon that ran alongside the road.

Sira, whose indifference to religion, according to Enrico, bordered on the sacrilegious, asked him why he bothered. "Is it that they're men of God? One would think God might situate them a bit closer to running water, no?" she teased, washing out Anna's turquoise dress on the back deck, enjoying the feel of the fresh water running through the clean, good cotton while Enrico pushed the mower over the lawn.

He shot her an annoyed look. "It's just that it's a nice thing to do, Sira, that's all. Doesn't cost me anything, and they're all a bit on the older side. Seems to me if a younger person can do something so that an older one doesn't have to troop up and down a mountain to get water, he should do it." Enrico valiantly attempted to keep mowing as he responded, but was doing a rather poor job of it.

"It must be so simple to be you sometimes, brother. To have such clear-cut rules."

She didn't mean it as a slight, however, and Enrico didn't take it as one. He looked up from the mower, a wayward strand of dark brown hair flopping into his face, and he beamed at her.

"Real easy, Sira. I have a know-it-all older sister for all the difficult, existential questions," he laughed, standing up abruptly when the lawnmower made a lurching motion as though making a break for it.

They'd coughed their way up the mountain ("This! Is not! A mountain!" Sira had exclaimed as they piled into the jeep, but Enrico and Anna, for whom the affair was an adventure of the grandest proportions, had steadfastly ignored her). Anna sat in Sira's lap, her amber-edged eyes taking in everything around her, pointing out the birds nesting high in the trees and the small, harmless snakes that slid into the moss on the sides of the road. Anna, Sira noted, was much more at home here than Sira herself had ever been, and the little girl had clung to Enrico's arm when he hoisted her up into the high front seat of the car.

The abbey was much more active than Sira had expected, with people both young and old milling about. Not many, Sira noted, were dressed in the garb of those who have taken religious vows. Enrico explained that the abbey hosted a religious retreat during the summer, taking advantage of the idyllic landscape that surrounded them. The money the pilgrims paid supported the priests in living their monastic lifestyle during the remainder of the year.

Anna tugged on her mother's shoulder, eyes wide.

"Mamma? That girl is wearing her *underwear*," she said, entirely scandalized.

Sira glanced over and noted that the twenty-something girl who was walking by, hand in hand with her more appropriately clad friend, was in actuality wearing a bathing suit, although not a particularly austere one, considering the location. The girls glanced appreciatively over their shoulders at Enrico unloading the barrels.

"Yes, my darling. It appears one does not want to be hindered by clothes while on a religious retreat," answered Sira dryly, earning a warning glance from her brother.

"I want to help, zio!" cried Anna, running over to the barrels. Enrico laughed.

"There's a good girl! How about you run in and tell one of the priests that we're here with lots of water for them?"

"They'll no doubt want to be filling a vat of water for those young girls, or else whatever are they in their swimsuits for?" Sira muttered, although she waited until Anna had scampered off to make the comment, and then went to help Enrico. The barrels were much too heavy for her to move. There were two of them, huge and made of oak, and Enrico wrestled the second one off the bed of the jeep, setting it upright before opening it so that he could show Sira the spring loading he had fashioned himself to facilitate opening and closing. Feeling the extreme heat of the day, he peeled off his shirt in an attempt to cool down.

"*Signor* Enrico!" someone called. "Sir, you dishonor us!"

Sira whirled to find a man in religious garb hurrying forward as fast as his sandaled feet would allow. He had one hand up high in the air and did not look very old to Sira, although his rotund shape implied he was not the most active of men. *Of course*, she thought, *if he has my brother running up and down the mountain for him, I can't imagine he has much use himself for exercise.* "Put your clothes back on immediately, sir! How dare you, in a place of worship!"

Sira's cat eyes narrowed as she took in the scurrying round, weak-chinned man. She glanced up at tall, handsome Enrico, now flushing a deep crimson from his neck. The priest reached the barrel and placed one hand on it in a proprietary manner. Enrico reached into the bed of the car for his shirt. Anna had reached him by then, wrapping her arms around one leg. She looked like she might cry. Enrico patted her blonde head briefly and then, almost in slow motion, head bowed, he swung his shirt around his shoulders, sliding one hand into a sleeve. Sira knew her brother, and knew that he was thinking hard—especially considering the presence of Anna, whose education in the ways of the world he considered of utmost importance.

"I do apologize, Father," he said firmly, deep baritone ringing.

The priest sniffed. *Don't get in the middle of this*, Sira told herself. *He's a fully grown man. He can protect himself.*

"I should hope so. I'll call to have someone come and get this water. I do hope that in the future, you will remain fully clothed when entering these premises."

When Sira saw her brother nod, she knew she wasn't going to be able to keep quiet. Ways of the world, indeed. "Which he won't be," she said, marching forward, barely containing her trembling.

The priest turned to face her for the first time. She had had just about enough. She walked over to him, seeming to grow from the lithe young woman she was to being roughly twice the size of the small, fat priest by the time she reached him. "My brother will never be doing you a favor again… Father. Not you, and not any of the other hypocrites."

The priest spluttered. Sira pointed, imperiously, back straight, toward the group of young people in varying degrees of undress.

"I cannot help but notice you have no ill words for them, man of God," she spat out. If the priest thought that her quiet voice was meant to be respectful, he was rather underestimating her. "But then again, they are paying you, while my brother is only bringing you water." And with that, she shoved the open barrel of water over onto the priest's feet.

He shrieked and jumped back.

Everyone in the courtyard stopped, staring at the reddening priest and this beautiful, scowling woman, and the only movement was that of the other priests running over from the shaded buildings. Sira, in the meantime, unlatched the other barrel, and despite her brother's quiet protest behind her, she tipped it over as well.

"If you need water, Father, by all means, go and get it yourself. No member of my family will ever be coming to your aid again. I trust your friends will be of assistance. I hope you've chosen well." Her tone was icy and supercilious, but underneath, her rage at these men and their disrespect of her brother was so great that she did not know if she could restrain herself. "And if I ever meet any of you on the road up the mountain again, I'll throw your fat little selves into the canyon!" *So much for keeping it together*, she thought.

She turned when she heard a noise behind her and found Anna, clapping her hands hard, tears running down her cheeks. Enrico looked mortified.

"Darling brother, could you grab those barrels, please?" she asked him smartly.

He did so without a word, loading them onto the bed of the jeep, and she thought she saw a smile playing on his lips.

"Signora, I am deeply…" the priest, prodded by another, had begun to speak.

Sira, who was helping Anna into the car once again, only turned to look him straight in the eye. "Father, with all due respect, please do shut up."

They had driven down the mountain with Anna chirping the whole way about how *brave* Sira was, and did zio see the look on that mean priest's face? Sira, who was starting to feel ashamed for having embarrassed her brother, felt a surge of relief when, while Enrico changed gears to tackle a difficult curve, he gently pressed the tip of his index finger on the back of her hand, just for a moment. Thank you.

It was a week later, while walking up the mountainous road chatting and having Anna point out the different types of flowers, that Sira saw two of the priests turn a corner on the road ahead. Anna froze and looked at her mother, and Sira did not like to see that she was afraid of the men. She grinned at her daughter, crooked an eyebrow in a conspiratorial expression, raised a delicately manicured hand, wiggled her fingers, and called out, "Yoooohooooo! You had best be running!" to the priests, who stopped dead when they saw her and then beat a hasty retreat. Anna burst into laughter and ran to take her mother's hand.

"Now, darling, what were we talking about?"

"Composure, mamma," Anna replied, looking up at her regal, dark-haired mother, who did not in any way seem like the sort of woman who would advise a priest to run from her.

"Ah yes, my love, of course. Composure. A most important trait. Shoulders back. Head up. Always. Even when you are alone. Especially when you are alone."

Chapter 8
Rome. Present day.

"We are going," Sira announced grandly, hands thrown up toward the living room ceiling, "on an *olive ascolane* mission."

"I can't eat fried foods," answered Little lazily, peering up at her aunt. She was spread out on the couch, attempting to glimpse the television behind her aunt's figure.

"I don't think it's legal to say that within the confines of this great nation, Little," countered Sira, taking the remote out of Little's hands and switching off the set. "And it's certainly better than sitting here and watching TV. Not to mention that olive ascolane are the specialty of a city, Ascoli Piceno, which sits proudly in a region of Italy called Marche, which you have undoubtedly never heard of." Little's raised eyebrows implied that Sira's assumption was indeed correct. "Exactly. It is time to spread your gastronomical wings. Also, they're delicious, and I just gave them a cultural context for you. Does that justify eating them?"

Little thought for a moment, felt her stomach rumble, nodded in acknowledgment, and sat up. "Yes. Yes, I think it does."

Despite it being almost an hour away on foot, and the sky a dull gray with the odd raindrop falling, they decided to walk to the restaurant in Trastevere, a particular favorite of Sira's thanks to the fact that they used extra virgin olive oil to fry. ("It's the only real oil, Little, and don't let anybody try to convince you otherwise," she said gravely as they walked out of the apartment.)

The air was clear and fresh, and the two women set a leisurely pace, looping the Colosseum and heading to Sira's favorite piazza: Piazza Trilussa.

"I never thought to ask you," said Little when they walked into the fairly plain square, "but why would Piazza Trilussa be your favorite in this entire city? There isn't really much here, not compared to lots of other piazze."

"Do you know who Trilussa was?" Sira asked. Little thought for a moment, then shook her head. "He was a Roman poet," Sira explained, "and he wrote in dialect. He was around, oh, end of the 19th century, beginning of the 20th, fairly recent. His last name was actually Salustri—the word Trilussa was an anagram."

"And? You like his poetry?"

"He wrote a poem called *La Tartaruga*. The Tortoise. Look it up sometime. It's very short. It's about an old turtle who over-steps one night and, falling, flips onto his back. While he's lying there, unable to get back on his feet, with his home underneath him, a toad yells out to him that he made a stupid mistake, that these errors cost *la pelle*, your skin. Your life. And the tortoise answers, I know. But at least before I die, I see the stars. *Prima de morì, vedo le stelle.*" Sira's eyes sparkled. "I have always loved that poem dearly. And so that is why I love this piazza, named after a man who made up his own name, and it doesn't seem so plain to me." She looked around and then nudged Little toward the small road to the right of the piazza that would lead them to the restaurant.

Flipping through the menu some time later, Little peeked cautiously over at the *olive* that the owner had proudly brought over to them almost immediately upon their sitting.

"*La signora Sira è sempre la benvenuta qui.*" *Madame Sira is always welcome here*, the large man had announced as soon as they had walked in, and Sira had preened slightly, making Little grin. Sira, knowing that Little was rarely enthusiastic about trying new things, looked over at her expectantly, nudging over one of the little round, golden balls on the plate in the center of the table. Little popped one in her mouth.

"Wow! These are great!" she said after chewing cautiously for a moment, and Sira rolled her eyes.

"Yes, well, I have excellent taste. Actually, I'm surprised you've never had these before."

"No, never! What are they? I taste olives, obviously."

"Green olives, stuffed with meat and then fried. They're named, like I had mentioned before, after the place they're from. Ascoli, *ascolane*."

Little picked up a few more and put them on her plate. Sira picked up a *supplì*, a fried rice ball, for herself, and while they ate Sira happily told Little about the importance of frying things lightly until Little remembered something she had wanted to ask Sira.

"Zia, the other day I was in Ostiense," she began. "I saw so many homeless people. Not that there aren't homeless people in San Francisco, but I don't remember seeing so many here before. And these people… Oh aunty, they were wrapped in blankets and asleep while the commuters marched by, inches away from their faces." She frowned. "Who *are* they?"

Sira, sighing, put down her food. "That question is more than I have an answer for. Why is anybody ever homeless? I suppose you could say that they are unwanted. From what I know of some of their stories, there are those that are Italians, honest people who can't pay the rent on the next-to-no pension they get after a lifetime of work, or who are simply unemployed. Of course, I'm generalizing here, but I think it is a common enough issue that I can do so. Some, more and more of them, come from other nations, places of war or persecution. I haven't seen seekers of solace in such numbers since the war, child…" Sira kept her eyes on the plate in front of her. "I thought I would never have to again." Little tucked her chair in closer to her aunt, one hand over hers.

"How much do you know about the war, Little?"

"What you've told me, what I've studied."

"Your dad was a little heathen during the war." Sira took a breath and looked at Little carefully. "Before my father moved us all to our country house in Narni, your father and his friends would steal food from the German trucks at night. You couldn't rein your father in; you couldn't just put a leash on him. You had to change his whole environment, or he would bulldoze right through whatever was in his way. But he did it with so much charm, you didn't even mind. I used to tell him that he better stop sneaking around at night or he wouldn't come back."

She sighed, shaking her head a little. "I thought that if I said it out loud I would make it not come true. I was powerful, even then. I realized early on that sometimes if I said things, I could make them happen, or make them not happen. So, when your father would sneak out at night, skinny gangly thing that he was, I'd grab him by the scruff of the neck and hiss that he'd better get into bed, that he'd never come back. That was how I tried to protect him. They used to make little cherry bombs out of things around the house—where they learned to do that I will never know—and they would set them off to distract the Nazis while they jumped in their trucks and stole their food. It used to drive the Nazis crazy. Your father always came home laughing, with food in his hands—the food the Germans kept for themselves, the meat and the good bread, not the black stuff they gave us Italians, the traitors. He always came back with his face smudged, his eyes alight with the adventure of it all. He didn't know how dangerous it was. None of us did. That's the truth. He wasn't being brave. He used to say to me that he'd never get hurt, because his older sister always made sure he came back safely."

She made an imploring face, her voice softening: "'Sira,' he'd whisper, and for a second his face would grow serious. 'I'm never afraid because I know you'd turn the world over for me.'"

For a moment, she paused, taking a sip of the water in front of her. "I would hiss at him to shut up, but oh, child, I would have. Even when he was little, your daddy knew how to make a person feel like they were the only ones in the whole wide world."

She looked at Little carefully, caught her confused expression. "I'm a silly old woman. Seeing you again reminds me so much of your father, and I suppose when you're old you tend to take your memories from further back." It did not seem to Little that Sira had been lost in memories. "Your father was a good man, Little. I suppose that's what I want to tell you."

"I know that, zia," cried Little. "Did you think I was doubting that because of what I asked you earlier, about Delila?"

"No."

There was a silence that Little felt was waiting for words not her own. She waited.

"Little," began Sira. Little looked up expectantly. "It's just that... I haven't seen you writing since you came back. Is something wrong?"

Little tried hard not to look frustrated. "Is that what you wanted to say?" She had the distinct feeling that what had come out of Sira's mouth had not been what she had initially meant to express.

"Just something I've noticed," Sira said. "It used to be so important to you."

"It still is." Little's expression became annoyed, and she stood from her chair. "I need to use the bathroom," she said over her shoulder as she strode off. When she turned the corner to the next room she glanced back, and the figure of her aunt sitting by herself at the table stamped itself into her mind, making her feel instantly guilty. She wanted to run back and hug the suddenly frail figure, but continued on. *There is definitely something important*, she thought as she turned a door handle, *that I am not supposed to find out.*

Chapter 9
Rome. 1983.

"Enrico, stop pacing, *per favore*. You're making me nervous."

Sira and Enrico were in the kitchen of the new house in Sperlonga, Enrico throwing open the large window that faced the woods so that the springtime air could drift in. His sister adjusted a cobalt-blue linen tablecloth she had found in the market that morning. "There. That's lovely, isn't it?" she said with satisfaction, stepping back from the table. "It rather suits the feel of the kitchen. Anyway, what's going on?"

"What do you mean?" answered Enrico nervously, opening a cabinet and rummaging inside. "Where's the *macchinetta?*"

"You mean the moka pot? Look on the bottom, to the right. I used it this morning."

"The moka pot. You're turning into an American, Sira," he laughed, pulling out the small coffeemaker and placing it on the old-fashioned stove.

"I love this place," said Sira, opening her arms wide to take in the lemon-yellow curtains, the wide windows, the trees bustling outside. "It feels like home."

Enrico nodded, spooning coffee into the machine. She eyed him carefully. "Not that I am not thrilled to be here and see your new home, but why exactly *am* I here? There's quite a lot going on in San Francisco at the moment I rather hoped not to miss, and I'm not sure you wanted me here only to pick out kitchen curtains. Although, frankly, I'm glad you did. I picked out fantastic ones." She grinned at her brother. "Enrico, you're white as a sheet. It does not go with the décor in this room. Whatever is the matter with you?"

"I'm getting married," Enrico finally said, keeping his eyes firmly on the stove. Sira's eyes widened slightly.

"Are you? I didn't even realize you were dating anyone."

"Yes, well. I'm marrying Delila Selinti."

"*What?*" Sira's jaw dropped. "Beppe Selinti's daughter?"

"Clearly. Do you know anyone else with his last name?"

"You are joking." She paused, looking at Enrico, clearly waiting for some sort of affirmation that he was, indeed, joking. He finally gave a tired shake of his head.

"Whatever for? You've never been the least interested in marriage, which I'll tell you, I've always found rather reassuring, because you're a bit of a mess."

Enrico raised one eyebrow. "I resent that."

"You don't." Sira waved her hands. "You know what I mean."

"Be that as it may. She's a nice girl."

"She's half your age."

"She's not half my age."

"Well, close enough. She told me when she turned thirty, you know. I remember going into her father's shop and her telling me. One thing I can do, thank goodness, is count."

Sira seemed to have lost her ability to focus, and she stared, brows furrowed, at Enrico's feet.

"What? What's wrong? For God's sake, Sira, can you please at least look at me?"

"Your shoes."

"My shoes?"

"What *shoes* are you wearing? Are those yellow?" Her expression was growing more horrified by the minute.

"They're mustard," Enrico clarified, smoothing out his pants. "The lady in the shop told me they're the very latest, and that I look dashing in them, if you must know. I bought them yesterday." He sniffed and raised his foot so that she could better see the dyed leather.

74

"Oh no, no, no, put your foot down." She covered her eyes with one hand and sighed. "Well this is the problem, isn't it," she gestured vaguely at Enrico's feet, "you'll let anybody convince you of anything!"

"You don't like them?"

"I would have to be color blind to like them." She grimaced at his expression. "Well, there's one good reason to marry into a family of merchants, I suppose. They can do something about your abominable taste in footwear." She could not help but make jokes, make her brother smile. "But *why*, Enrico? Honestly, this doesn't make any sense. You're not interested in her at all, you never have been! Is that Beppe blackmailing you?" She had expected Enrico to protest, but put up a hand when Enrico opened his mouth. "Do not lie to me. I know better. I know you, at least. Tell me what this is all about. You've always been much too nice to that creaky Selinti fellow, and he's always been horrible to you. I've always thought it was strange that you kept going back to their shop. The girl is nice, I'll give you that much, but come on. This is crazy!" She reached over and squeezed her brother's arm.

"I... I have to."

"You have to." Sira echoed. Enrico nodded, and Sira felt flush with protectiveness.

"I have no choice."

"There is *always* such a thing as a choice."

Enrico put a hand to his forehead, frowned. "No. Not if you're a decent person. There are rules to abide by if you're a decent person."

Sira rolled her eyes. "Enrico, don't be ridi—"

"Sit down, sister." He placed a heavy hand on Sira's shoulder, gestured to one of the oak chairs he had picked out the week before. "There are things you need to know."

Chapter 10
Rome. Present day.

There were pages everywhere. Little generally enjoyed such a state of affairs, but in this case it did not seem to make anything better at all. She, Anna, and Sira were all standing in the living room of the apartment in Rome after Sira had announced that the place needed, as she put it, "a thorough upheaval." So far this had yielded nothing but scraps of paid bills, old opera playbills, and sticky notes with unknown numbers scrawled across them in Enrico's handwriting.

"What about the safe?" asked Anna. Little had forgotten about the safe, a most mysterious object about the size of a large cardboard box that her father had always kept in a reinforced cabinet of the living room, saying only that he kept his valuables there. She had never looked, of course.

"I don't know the combination," she said.

Sira shrugged. "I looked in the cabinet some time ago, but all I found were some watches and a few other valuables. They were arranged on top of the safe instead of inside it, which I thought was strange. Remember I sent you one of the gold watches, Little? Anyway, I never looked inside the safe. I don't know the combination, either."

Anna smiled, smug. "I do," she said, opening the cabinet door and leaning down. Little rolled her eyes, but only once she knew Sira wasn't looking.

Anna swung open the heavy metal door and pulled out a sheaf of papers, looking confused. She laid them out on the table. "Are these... are these children's drawings?"

Little walked over and picked up the yellowed pages, messy crayon drawings wrapped in plastic wrap that was taped into submission on the back of the drawing. And now she remembered being six years old and convinced she was going to be an artist.

She had spent hours and hours leaning over the table on the patio, drawing her favorite orca whales, their tails always carefully flipped in the same direction even if they were meant to be underwater, their black and white spots just so. Then she had instructed Sira on exactly how the paper needed to be covered in plastic wrap to achieve a professional, laminated sheen, before being carefully slipped into an oversized envelope and posted back to Italy, to the same apartment she stood in now. After six months or so of being a veritable orca-drawing machine, she had dropped the whole project and promptly forgotten about the drawings and her vocation. Now, she saw there were at least a dozen of them, enough to fill his little safe.

She looked up to see Anna tugging the rest of the pages roughly from inside the small enclosure, running her hand around the metal sides and checking that there was nothing else before impatiently slamming her hand on the top of the box. She threw the drawings onto the table, her eyes darting from one end of the table to the other, as though convinced the safe had held something hidden, something that had fallen out.

"What's your problem?" Little asked harshly. She knew she was being cold with her cousin, but Anna's aggressive demeanor permeated the whole house and Little didn't feel like playing into what she felt were Anna's attention-getting tactics. Anna's eyes were so angry when she looked up that Little took a step back.

"I don't have a problem, Little. But I don't understand why zio treated a toddler's scribbles as though they were made of gold, and left things of actual value out where anybody could take them."

"I mean, first of all, those aren't scribbles, they're quite good," Little wondered for a moment why she was defending her six-year-old self's artistic ability. "And I guess that depends what you consider things of actual value. You were pretty upset about that Pinocchio doll the other day. But I guess that was different, right? It's just not okay if it's something that has to do with me, that reminds you that he loved me, too, that I'm his daughter." Little replied in frozen tones, gathering the scattered pages and stacking them neatly in a pile, focusing her attention on the blues and greens of the old pictures to avoid looking Anna in the face. She wanted to be strong and grown-up, but instead she could feel the resentment growing hot in her throat, threatening to spill onto her cheeks. *Look at what I did for this family. I left my world to come back to this family, so stop being so bitter!* But that didn't sound right, either, and for some reason, Little did not trust herself to speak just then.

"Such an upstanding member of this family. Picked up and left right after he died. Poor Little, her daddy died and she just couldn't hack it." Little wanted to sneer coolly at Anna's words but felt her stomach turn hotly.

"Girls, please. Why are you so upset? It wasn't a competition. Love isn't a thing you compete over…" Sira stepped in between them and looked as though she had more to say, but suddenly stopped. "It isn't a thing you compete over." She repeated slowly. Anna sidestepped her mother; there was a moment when her eyes locked with Little's, and Little was certain the poisonous words from after Enrico's funeral would erupt again. She felt a sudden sense of, not loneliness, but a cavernous denseness that she couldn't name.

"Oh Anna, don't," she heard Sira say, and then the slam of the front door. Sira looked at Little, bereft.

"Maybe she'll come back?" Little ventured.

"I don't know if you noticed, but she's a touch uncompromising." Sira tried to smile.

"No idea where she got it from."

Sira picked up the phone and dialed. Little stayed long enough to make sure Anna picked up, and then walked to her bedroom. Anna's words had catapulted her back to that time when her father was sick, just before he'd died. Once he'd been moved to the hospital, it had taken her a long time to venture into his studio. When she had found the courage, she had walked down to the garage of the home in Sperlonga, rolling back the doors as he had loved to do; he had never wanted anything closed. She had found out at some point that he had been massively claustrophobic, but she thought she could understand that, too. He had not feared closed spaces, just craved open ones. She had walked down there and tried to tell herself that he would get better, that he would sit at the worktable he had made for himself and build things, fix everything. She did not want to be here, not where he had been so fiercely alive, such a contrast to the hollowed-out man in the hospital bed. *Even then,* she thought, *even there he'd been a lion,* and she flushed with belated, angry pride.

It was there, on the table, a half-built miniature of a boat. An outline. Everything else had been cleared out, although she didn't know by whom, or when.

"*È rimasta solo la forma di una barca,*" Sira had told her. *All that's left is the shape of a boat.* His last project, before the chemotherapy had made him too weak to walk down here from the main house. Before she had returned to this country she still felt no connection to. She placed her hands gently on the wood and imagined him standing in the same place as she was now, but with intent. *Why were you building this, papà?* she thought fiercely, angrily. She wanted to sweep it off the table and watch it break. She wanted to put it somewhere safe and keep it forever, this last passion project of a father who was never going to see his daughter fully grown. She wanted to destroy it, she wanted to cherish it.

She remembered then a time when she was still little, and he had decided that she must learn how to swim. Despite her aunt's concerned voice telling him that children should learn how to swim in a pool, in a safe environment, he had swept her off to the sea. No daughter of mine learns how to swim in a pool, he had said, laughing.

"You have to kick, kiddo." He'd let her go, and in the turbulent, dark water, the presence of his hand poised to catch her had fallen just short of being any sort of reassurance.

Only when she was near the sea could she feel his presence. She had reached the same beach where he had taught her years before. He would take her here, every time he wanted to talk to her, until the end of his life, as if he did not know how to relate to this girl child without the sand under his toes to give him strength. Unconsciously, he had passed this on to her, too, this desperate need to recalibrate confusions within by the drumming of the waves.

It was empty, the biting weather serving as a deterrent. "Where are you?" she yelled out, but the sea only murmured back, indistinguishable. "By all means, no straight answers," she muttered. She turned her back meanly, planning to forsake their tradition of always touching the water. She made it halfway back to her car before the pressure grew too great and she whirled, running back, until she knelt at the edge, breathing hard, waiting for the rushing water to run over her splayed hands. It didn't make her feel as much better as it should have, but it was a little bit of a good thing, and that was enough.

I'm afraid that I have nothing left to say. Nothing worth hearing. Nothing to tie together. She considered, for the first time, sitting by the sea that she knew had in some way done its part to raise her, that her assumptions had abandoned her, and she wondered if it wouldn't be rather nicer to have them back.

She never went back there. She didn't have time for it, she had told herself. There are such a lot of things to do, of dreams to deny. Sometimes, when she slipped down the antiseptic hallway of the hospital, or in the moment she leaned over to turn the light on, the thoughts would glide in. Why are there steps, and where do they lead? And why do they not follow a straight path upward? What assurances did she have? This should be done in leaps and bounds, under a clear blue sky with the sunshine pouring down, for strength. She should be able to fly.

But she still looked for the sea whenever she could. And when the birds cried overhead, she automatically scanned the skies for the gulls, her eyes holding longing.

After he had died, she had been to the grave but felt that there was nothing there. Not just nothing, but an empty space, a negative summation of the man who had not always been perfect but had, in fact, always been her father. She had tried to write a story afterward, of the type that had poured out of her since she had been a little girl. She wanted to write of a fully grown, sturdy boat bobbing gently along the coast of the Tyrrhenian, miles and maybe even years away. Nobody knew where it had come from, but there it was, watertight and secure. It looked as though it could carry all manner of things safely through deep waters.

Or those were the words Little had whispered to herself when she woke up one morning soon after he had died. She never wrote it down. She had left Italy the next day.

Chapter 11
Rome. Present day.

Little wasn't sleeping. Or at least, she wasn't sleeping particularly well, a fact easily attributed to her insistence on keeping up with her friends in San Francisco and thereby staying firmly on West Coast time. No matter how many times she told herself that this didn't have to be a permanent move, and that the faster she moved forward the better off she'd be, the urge to count back nine hours always got the best of her. On the seventh day of her stumbling into the kitchen well past noon, Sira had looked up from her coffee with a discerning gleam in her eye.

"I think," she had begun, in a tone that Little knew preceded a suggestion which was not actually up for discussion, "that it is time you look up Barbara and reestablish some friendships here. Get acclimated. I'm not seeing a lot of acclimation."

"Right," Little sighed. "Well," she said as she glanced down at her flip-flops, which Sira had been starting to stare at with something that resembled deep dissatisfaction, "I've been wanting to head to the artisan leather shops in the streets around Piazza di Spagna so I can get some decent sandals." She wiggled her toes.

"Oh, finally! Uh, I mean, I think that sounds like a fantastic idea." And she had gone back to her espresso.

Which was how Little found herself setting out for Piazza di Spagna the next morning, stifling her yawns. She meandered toward the metro, grimly hoping that she would miss rush hour, although she was beginning to consider quite seriously that Rome was made up of one long rush hour of more or less intense variations. She tried not to think about her father's pages. She knew that she would have to go back to his house in Sperlonga if she wanted to find anything of similar importance, and after what had happened with Anna the last time she did not feel ready to take on any more memories. So she had decided to put the whole thing out of her mind, which so far had, of course, ensured only that she was always, in some way, thinking about it.

Running down the steps of the old metro station, she realized she was quite late, and despite the constant jokes of lateness being written into the Italian bloodstream, she did not like not being on time. Of course, nobody in the station was moving faster than a morose turtle, and Little quickly became frantic with impatience, so much so that she wasn't even looking around, and didn't notice him until she was all the way down to the platform—and then only because his bright green shirt caught her eye. He had enough charisma to persuade a herd of elephants—you could tell that from miles away—which, Little thought, they may as well be with all of the people in between them.

The sign hanging from the roof of the station flashed that they had three more minutes before the next train came, time that Little spent trying to get a good look at the man while respecting the general metro rule of never actually looking at anybody else. Some people just ooze glamour, even in the middle of a sweaty station in the hottest spring Rome had seen since last spring. Despite the people around him, the man stood slightly apart, reserved, a gentle frown bending his eyebrows toward each other. The older lady next to him was attempting to sidle closer, causing him to have to continuously sidestep her. She was wearing the dark brown leather bag that seems to be a staple of the agreed uniform of the more senescent of society. He glanced at it apprehensively, and for a moment Little had one of those flashes that tells you that you're having the same thoughts as the person you're looking at. She wanted to smooth his frown out with her fingers.

She was still looking at him sideways when the metro came screaming into the station, and, muscles suddenly clenched, without looking straight ahead, the man in the green shirt stepped out past the yellow line and leaned out over the gap, as though listening for something. There was no dramatic leaping, nothing to warn the bystander that here was something that should be noticed.

Little barely had time to open her mouth. Her scream hadn't even formed by the time the train hit him.

Little's thoughts froze, came in bursts; she no longer remembered where she had been in such a hurry to get to. She placed her hand gently against the side of the stopped train to steady herself, and thought she felt the metal underneath shaking, throbbing, although the machine itself was now deathly still. She could see the man's hands down on the tracks, palms outstretched, reaching, the only part of his body whose movement remained gentle, unviolated.

She must have leaned forward slightly, because one of the station guards, who were suddenly everywhere, slammed her backward as though she were about to jump in there after him. She wasn't. She could see through the pale flesh of his hand, as though his lifeline had come unzipped and the rest of him had fallen out.

Afterward, she thought that if truth worked a different way, then maybe if you had to see someone die there would be flashes of color during the unpleasant bits, pieces of the story intertwined inside a person. He loved jasmine when it bore flower in the early summer, could smell it before he saw it, so a light amethyst might do; sunsets, so a dazzling citrine. When his son was born, he walked around seeing fireworks for days on end, flying up past the Colosseo. When he was lonely, he looked up at the darkening sky: sapphire. Tumbling gems, everywhere.

Or maybe not. Maybe some things are meant to not be pretty.

Little had heard somewhere that in order to force yourself to function, the easiest, the only, thing to do is focus on the next immediate task. So she instructed her left foot to take a step, and then her right foot to follow, and repeated those two orders to herself numbly until she found herself outside again. She looked around at the buzz all around her, people walking and running and talking, and she wondered, not for the first time, how the world could still be moving. She stared down at the ground, then swung her neck up until she could see the sky. A middle-aged woman with her hair pulled back in a tight bun was crossing the street, a smear of something that might have been gelato across her cheek. Little blinked, and realized the sound she was hearing was her phone ringing.

"Barbara? I'm sorry I'm late. The metro's stopped."

"Little?" came the familiar sound of Barbara's voice. "What's wrong? You sound terrible."

"Nothing. I'll walk there." She did not know how to say, *I just saw a man die.*

"Where are you? I'm coming to pick you up in my car. Just stay there." Her voice was worried. Little looked around.

"I'm in Piazza Re di Roma, at the metro stop." She could practically hear Barbara starting her car.

"Just hold on, I'm on my way," she said. *I am,* thought Little. *I am holding on.*

***

Barbara was there in less than fifteen minutes, leaving Little to wonder about how many shortcuts she had taken, and she scooped Little up in her tiny compact car, which she'd had painted a violent shade of bright blue. She gave Little a long hug, then swung her long chestnut hair behind her, yelled at the car behind her to stop honking, and swung back into traffic.

While she questioned Little about what had happened on the metro, Little remembered how impossible it was to be unhappy around Barbara, whose petite frame belied an entirely rambunctious, but also surprisingly thoughtful, personality. Her family owned the beach house across the street from Little's in Sperlonga. The two girls had inherited their friendship from their fathers, who had been fast friends since they had shared buckets of paint with each other while building their homes.

"Let's go get a *caffè*," Barbara said as she parked, and she led Little deep into the tiny cobblestoned streets off of the Piazza di Pietra in the historical center.

After having walked by three restaurants, Little finally ventured, "Couldn't we stop in one of these? I mean, isn't it all the same?"

Barbara cocked her head. "It's coffee! Of course it's not all the same. You've been gone too long. Anyway, we're here," she finished, and sat herself in one of the chairs haphazardly set around the tables outside a tiny café. Little sat down across from her and smiled. It really was good to see her friend.

"How have you been?" she tried, but Barbara gave her the same straightforward look Little had begun to associate with Italian women.

"You said two words in the car, Little. And am I wrong, or did you just see some poor soul end his life?" Little flinched visibly. "Don't pretend it just didn't happen. Talk to me."

"Barbara, I want to hear about you. It's been too long."

"All the time in the world," Barbara shrugged, calling over the waiter and ordering two *caffè shakerati*, the frothy cold coffee drink favored by the Italians in the warmer weather. "That's definitely what you want," she assured Little just before ordering. "What happened?" she said to her friend again, gently.

"You know," Little started, "I didn't know it would be important. I don't even remember. I wasn't paying *attention*. Or I was, but not enough. Not to that. I didn't even know who he was." As soon as she said it she realized it was a silly thing to say, because how could she have possibly known who he was, or known anybody who had been there? They were all in the same place simply because they were all going somewhere else at the same time. "He had a wry, lopsided smile," she continued, recalling his face, Barbara's clear gaze unwavering on her own, "and a green shirt, floppy brown hair. That's all I know. And it's just not enough. It's just not enough about a person." Barbara took her hands and placed them on Little's, as though to give her strength to keep talking. "I'll read about him in the newspaper. They do throw that stuff in sometimes, if it's particularly gory or time-consuming, which it will be. I'm sure the metro will be stopped for hours. They told us to leave the station. I'll hear the usual stories, maybe about how he couldn't pay the bills, or his wife had left him, sick kid, did you hear he lost his job? And I won't know which stories are true, which boxes he checked that would either make it okay or add him to a list of causes he could be slid into. The economy, a lack of concern for citizens, the color of the sky, or the running of trains on tracks and what happens when they careen off them…" She only grew aware of the tears on her cheeks when the waitress with their coffee stared at her as she put the little plates down before putting one hand very lightly on Little's shoulder as she walked away. It occurred to Little, who was surprised at how shocked she was, that it was more than likely no one would have done that in America. Space. There was so much more space in America. Nobody would ever touch a stranger, especially not a customer—it just wasn't acceptable. And yet that touch, unplanned, when the other girl had no idea what Little could be upset about, moved her deeply. She didn't want space and roles just then. She wanted people who would be sorry just for the fact that there were tears on her face, and who would not fear showing that to her.

Barbara scooted her chair in closer so she could wrap Little in another hug. "You wish that what a newspaper story told you could be different, right?"

She folded a napkin, this friend who had never once said no when they were children and Little wanted to go exploring. When twelve-year-old Little had broken her ankle climbing a fence on one of those adventures, Barbara had covered for her and told an angry Sira that Little had indeed tripped down the stairs. She had brought over gelato every evening for the rest of that summer, and when Little couldn't bear to be stuck inside anymore, she had slung Little's arm over her shoulders and walked her to the beach so that they could sit by the water. Now, she carefully dabbed the smeared mascara from Little's cheeks.

"You want to know what books he liked to read, if he had dimples when he smiled outright, if he cried openly or if he was one of those people who wiped his nose on his coat. If he loved his job or was it just about bringing the money home, was he nervous around planes, secretly had he wanted to be a journalist or an adventurer or a pirate? Had cats made him sneeze, and if he had to say whom he had loved the most then could he have told you?" Barbara finished, the end of a sad smile shadowing her face.

I have good friends here in Italy, Little thought suddenly. *Strong friends.*

"Yes. That's… That's exactly it." Suddenly Little wanted to know what was going on with her friend, didn't want to keep on being sad. "Barbara, I really, really want to hear about you."

"I want to talk about this!" Barbara exclaimed.

"We can talk about it! But I've missed you. I haven't seen you in such a long time, and I want to hear about what's up with you, in person, not over the phone or through email." Little took a sip of her *caffè shakerato* and made a mental note to remember it was delicious for next time. "I know you were looking for a job?" Barbara had studied pedagogy, but had so far found the search for steady employment to be a challenge.

Barbara shrugged.

"Well, you know I grew up studying ballet, so now I'm teaching dance at an academy. It works. I mean, I'm living at home, because I can't afford an apartment of my own, but it's my mom and me, and she's great. I don't mind."

Little frowned. It was rather clear that she did. "It's great that you're teaching dance, but I thought you wanted to teach? As in, something different?"

"I do, I just can't find a job. And this pays the bills while I keep looking. Honestly, it isn't like specialized work pays much more than what I make now. What I really wanted to do was open a kindergarten for children with special needs." Barbara's voice became animated, and she opened her arms. "I knew I couldn't do that right away, but I thought if I got some experience, then eventually I could do it."

"Why can't you? That sounds like an incredible idea, completely worth pursuing!" Little exclaimed, but Barbara only shrugged again.

"I know, but I can't even find a job teaching, so how can I ever get to the point of opening a school? Plus, with all the bureaucratic red tape to even start anything, much less a business, I'd have to have connections…"—here she raised a hand way above her head and wiggled her fingers—"…way up here."

"Who cares about connections? You can do it anyway, you just have to work hard."

"No, Little. It doesn't work that way here. It just doesn't. It isn't *I work hard and get somewhere.*" Barbara's voice grew anxious. "It's *I work hard, and I can't even find a job unless I have enough money to start with and know the right people.*"

"I'm sorry, I didn't know. I didn't mean to sound obnoxious."

"No, I'm not mad at you. I'm not. I'm mad…" She looked around and continued, "I'm mad at how dysfunctional this place is but how much I love it, anyway."

"I think that's the biggest difference I see between here and back ho—" Little caught herself. "San Francisco, I mean. San Francisco swaggers. The young generation there… they're certain that they are, or in some way can and will be, successful. That their ideas are inherently valuable. And every time I come back here, I'm shocked by the angry lack of hope in people our age. And I think, as grating as that American swagger can be sometimes, don't the Americans have every right to feel a sense of entitlement toward their own success? Shouldn't Italy be able to gift this feeling to its young as well?"

Little was speaking to Barbara, but voicing a question she had had for a long time.

"Those are nice thoughts, Little. They really are. If we could make it better, we would, you know. But how? The money isn't flowing. We have overpaid politicians and underpaid everybody else." Barbara answered, her voice suddenly very sad.

Little looked back at her friend. She had no answer. Unbidden, she thought of her father, writing about starlings, about little Giacomo running through the streets of his neighborhood, his world, a world whose hold was precarious.

"Come on," Barbara said, getting up with a start. "Enough with all this serious talk. I need to remind you why it's a *good* thing that you're here!"

"Where are we going?"

"Sermoneta. The stone city lost in time." She waggled her eyebrows. "We can take my car."

***

Sermoneta seemed all made of light-colored stone, moss-green trees, and the twinkling sound that comes from water splashing lightly against the bottom of a fountain. Barbara walked deftly up the stairs leading to an entryway that seemed to be made of rock, and when Little reached the top she caught a flash of sun against a small, bronze-colored fountain. *Water and flame*, she thought to herself. She could see now what Barbara had meant by saying the city was lost in time—it was more than easy to imagine herself a lady of the past, walking down these streets in search of adventure or refuge. She hurried to keep up with her friend's bobbing figure as she pointed to the huge fortress in the background that seemed to guard the tiny streets sprouting every which way.

"That is the castle of the Caetani noble family. It was originally built as a military fortress, which is why it looms like that. It's the main chess piece of the center." As they talked, Barbara, who seemed to know exactly where she was going, had veered down an incline, past another small piazza, and turned left into a small, open doorway. Little followed her in and discovered a low-lit, high-ceilinged room with a beautiful wooden chandelier hanging above and paintings, which seemed to be predominantly blue, adorning the walls. An elegant woman with a pixie cut was bustling toward them, her arms open.

"Barbara!" she called, and Barbara threw her own arms open in response.

"Maryna! This is a close friend of mine, Little," she said, bending toward Maryna for a kiss. "Little, this is Maryna, who owns this gorgeous restaurant." The woman laughed, hugged Barbara, and then kissed Little on both cheeks while shaking her hand.

"Welcome, both of you! Barbara, do you want your usual table outside? It's fantastic weather for the view, and no one is sitting there at the moment." Barbara nodded and Maryna led them outside to a tiny table tucked next to a low stone parapet overlooking part of the castle and then opening to the hills below. A bunch of flowers in varying vibrant shades of pink decorated the low wall, and a bright yellow butterfly was hovering over the petals.

"Is this real life?" Little ventured, and Barbara threw back her head and laughed, delighted.

"Welcome to Sermoneta, Little. I do hope you're hungry."

***

Little had never had her meat cooked in quite such a succulent way. She gleefully forked yet another mouthful of the sweet red onion compote that perfectly accentuated the taste of the veal. Maryna came over several times to check on them, her bright blonde hair weaving through the people who had come to find sustenance after a long day of exploring. Little tasted Barbara's dish, a specialty spaghetti of the house made with ricotta and almonds, and wondered if she should simply finish this meal and start over again. For dessert, Maryna recommended a *semifreddo* made with tart oranges, which Little inhaled. A delighted Maryna pointed out an orange tree down the minute, cobbled street that bordered the restaurant.

"The oranges come from that tree, and my mother made the marmalade to top the semifreddo," she announced proudly, laughing uproariously when Little wondered aloud whether Maryna's mother might possibly agree to come back to Rome and live in Little's house, making as much marmalade as she wanted.

When they left quite a long time later, after they had lingered over coffee and filled their eyes with the turrets of the castle and the surrounding hills, Maryna hugged both Little and Barbara. The two women walked slowly back to the car, enjoying the quiet, muted grandeur of the tiny, ancient city. Little looked over at Barbara, who had her face tilted up in order to catch the slowly dying sunlight. She looked pensive as she beeped her car open and slid into the driver's side.

"Speaking of the Caetani," she began as she turned the ignition, "the family once created a splendid garden not far from here. It weaves throughout the ruins of a medieval village known as Ninfa, a name dedicated to the nymphs. The last woman of the Caetani family, Lelia, was a painter, and it was her vision that guided the renewal of the garden during her last years. It's fed by three sources of water, one of which is the river of Ninfa, which flows under the bridges that span the water, past the bamboo grove and the tree that cools its red roots in the river. The plants are from all over the world, and there are uncountable species of birds." When Barbara said the word birds, her hands fluttered from the steering wheel for a moment, into the air. "You know, it's open to the public now, though only a few days a year. I'll take you one day, when we can see the flowers flushed with color. I'll show you the ruins of the main church of the village, where you can still see the frescoes etched onto the old walls, though the plants have almost overrun them. We can go to the secret pool in the middle of the bamboo grove, and you can drink from it. The rumor, of course, is that nymphs still live there."

"Is that real?" Little asked for the second time that day. "Is there really a place like that?"

Barbara turned to her, one eyebrow raised so high it disappeared underneath her bangs. "Would I joke about anything that important?"

"I feel... better," she ventured, and this time Barbara smiled, satisfied.

"Of course. Places like that," she said, inclining her head toward the city they were leaving behind, "are salves, and wonders. Places to see and never to forget." Turning to her friend with a grin, she continued, "See, Little, we're not just a lost country. You just have to get to know us."

Which gave Little an idea.

Chapter 12
Rome. 1995.

Delila ran through the streets of Rome, searching, searching. The day was balmy and relaxed, people strolling the streets as though they had not a care in the world, but Delila didn't notice the weather or the mood. She was furious, so angry she felt her blood run hot and her vision turn dark. As she ran she held a letter tightly in her hand, the pages crumpling and jutting out from her fist. On the very edge, if someone had looked carefully, they would have been able to make out a symbol scribbled on the corner of the envelope.

Where was he? He had left that morning, saying he was taking their daughter to Piazza Mattei. She loved the fountain that sat in the middle of the piazza, the one with the little stone turtles scrambling their way up to the top, hoisted by the stone men below them.

Anger, resentment, fear rose up in her throat, a bile she couldn't swallow away. A wasted life, thrummed her footsteps as she turned the streets over, a monotonous rhythm as her feet hit the pavement. *Your wasted life, your wasted life.* She wanted to scream. She wanted to hurt somebody, wanted to rip her eyes out for not ever having seen.

She tore into the piazza, and there they were, making up an idyllic scene without her: her husband, the man she loved fiercely, one hand tucked into his pocket, strong shoulders and dark hair outlined by the sun. He was chatting to a couple just outside of a café, coffee cup in his hand, keeping one careful eye on their little girl, who was standing outside of the range of the fountain, playing some form of skipping game with a little boy who looked to be about her age. Delila's mouth twisted. She was no longer able to see anything past the lies.

When Enrico saw her, she was already halfway across the piazza. His eyebrows lifted slightly at her expression, and he walked to meet her. As she approached him, she threw the letter at him, and his act of catching it in his hand infuriated her even more. It should *hurt* to have the truth slammed into you.

"I *found* this with my father's things," she snarled. He looked down at the envelope, and his face paled.

"*Aspetta*, Delila…" he began, and when she went to answer him she instead found herself screaming, her mouth wide open. She snatched the letter back out of his hand. Out of the corner of her eye, she saw her daughter turn around and begin to walk over, then halt when Enrico put one hand out to her.

"*Amore, un momento*," he called out to her. The words resounded in her head. *Amore, amore, amore.*

"*Ti odio*, Enrico," she hissed, and found there were no other words that she could say, that they were all cramming themselves into her throat, desperate to fling themselves out at him, blocking each other so that anger ravaged her face. She looked up at him. Hadn't she always loved how tall he was, how she had to tilt her head back to take in his face?

His eyes were sad but calm, and she hated him for that. If he had ever loved her, surely there would have been turmoil there. "Did you ever feel *anything*," she said finally, quietly, not a question, registering the quiet defeat in his eyes. She would show him. She would make him care. Force him. The only sign of real panic was in the way his hands were reaching out for their tiny child. Out of the corner of her eye, Delila could already see Enrico's sister turning the corner into the piazza. That meddling woman. How was she always around? Here was why her daughter never paid attention to her own mother, always and only looking for Sira. No one in this family was ever looking for Delila.

With a jerk, Delila turned and flew toward the little girl, feeling her anger turning into a ball of iron in her stomach, an entity so physical she could feel it shoving her forward.

"Delila, *non fare scemenze*." *Don't do anything stupid.* Enrico started toward the place where the little girl was standing, frozen in fear, not knowing what was wrong but knowing, without a doubt, that something was. But Delila was closer, and though she had not known what she would do when she reached the girl, the years of feeling unloved piled up within her. She felt fiercely validated: she had been *right* all those times she had felt as though he were detached, physically present but vacant. He *hadn't* loved her. It had all been untrue. Everything. Her marriage, her father, her own baby. They had taken away the life she had imagined for herself. She flung her arm out, her hand stretched open. She wanted to turn around and *see* Enrico's reaction.

The slap was heard around the piazza, everyone suddenly frozen in their place. The moment that Delila's hand had touched the child's cheek, all of her energy had drained out of her.

She did not feel Enrico yank her child away from her, did not hear Sira's furious hiss behind her. Delila, for the first time in many years, blissfully felt nothing.

Chapter 13
Rome. Present day.

When the sky hung so gray and ominous that it felt like a blanket enveloping the city, Sira walked herself over to the Terme di Caracalla, the haunted open-air ruins of the Roman emperor of the same name. These ancient, grandiose public bath houses only bore his name because he was emperor when they were finished, so Sira always felt that naming them after him had been somewhat unfair. But then, she supposed, empires weren't built on fairness. Grand they certainly were, she had to admit, even now that they were not what they had been built to be. What was now a sepia-toned skeleton had once been a meeting place of the ancient Romans, a point of recreation. The tawny remains of the massive structure broke high into the sky so that Sira had to tilt her head back to take them in. She had always found these ruins to be so dignified that every time she passed she wondered if the whole of them, thousands of years past, could have possibly been more awesome than they were now, or if they were always meant to reach their greatest grandeur as relics. She had always appreciated and been awed by gargantuan displays such as this one, big gestures impossible to misunderstand.

She stood in the field that stretched before the high, fractured walls, resting one long-fingered hand on the trunk of the holm oak that guarded this corner of the strip of soil separating the ruins from the traffic. She mused that only in the cities would one describe this little patch of green as a field. But if kids could play soccer on it, in city terms it was a field, and so that was the way Sira thought of it, though the vast plains of the Umbrian countryside intermingled with the wild expanses of unbroken California moors in her own definition of what land could be.

There was no one here, of course, not with a storm coming, and the proud figure of the slight, older woman cut against the golden shading of Caracalla. She steadied herself against the bark of the tree, taking in the tentative, new green of its leaves, waiting to feel a presence, to sense an order to the things that were swirling around her little family. When enough pressure had built up inside her, Sira looked firmly up at the threatening expanse of sky and began to speak.

"How could you take him away from me?"

The words startled her; that had not been what she had meant to say. "How could you take him away," she repeated softly, knowing she was talking to herself. "Nobody told her the truth. I *told* him to, but I protected him when he didn't. I'm just as much at fault. And now... now it's more complicated for her."

A great rage filled her then, an anger that had been purling in the corners of her gut for too long, the mercurial frustration of helplessness. The wind was picking up, trying to lift her silver hair but finding it too thoroughly hair-sprayed to have much of an effect. For a moment, she thought of what a sight she must be, a minute, old lady standing under a tree, yelling to what was rapidly becoming only darkness. *Old lady my foot*, she thought to herself, and straightened her back despite the pain that clung to her hips and spine almost constantly these days. The ruins cast long, creeping fingers over the grass, and the birds had stopped singing when the wind had begun its sharp, whistling song.

"How can I help her? Is it too late to tell her? Surely it's best if this all remains uncovered. What can I change now, anyway? So many years ago." If Sira had been the sort of human who yelled when she was angry or lost, she would have been screaming now; instead, she was the type who grew quieter the more menacing she felt, and if the universe had known what was good for it, it would have feared her whispers. Instead, air swirled around her as the rippling grass lent texture to the lengthening shadows, and Sira still did not know what to do.

Had the ground not been so muddy and seemed so far off, Sira was quite certain she would have settled herself unceremoniously on the damp earth and taken a rest there. She gazed at one of the ancient markers of the city, at the orange tape that festooned the low, flimsy aluminum gate that surrounded this part of the Terme. She realized that she had thought it natural that her city would protect her niece, a child of its borders, that it would enchant her enough to pull her out of a reverie of a lost father and a place she had called home, but which, in fact, was not.

The roots of the tree grew tangled and looked like bone against the dark dirt in the feeble light of failing evening. Sira knew that the city that had watched the betrayal and death of empires, senators, gladiators, and paupers was not likely to overly concern itself with a lost little girl. Then, for the first time, her eyes focused on the roots of the tree, and she bent down to touch, to feel, rubbing the dirt beneath her fingers. The thought came to her then that instead of the bleached bone that had come unbidden to her mind at first sight, these deep and life-giving twists reminded her of arteries.

The rain began to fall, pattering slowly at first and then picking up speed and vehemence, and Sira was grateful that the breath-holding moments of waiting for the water were over.

***

A map of Italy was laid out on the living room table, one of the old ones with faded colors and undecided outlines. Its corners bent in toward the center, and the crease in the middle was so overly worn that it was unthinkable for the map to bend any other way, or to see the names of the cities that had been scrubbed off in the folds. Little had found it among her father's things and was standing over it, hands on her hips, lips curled in thought, when Sira let herself into the apartment. She smiled to herself when she saw Little's eyes alight with excitement, and sidled over to stand next to her. She put one finger on the circle that identified the capital.

"I was thinking I might take a trip," Little began, looking over at her aunt anxiously in the hopes of reading her expression, worried she would be against it. "I still have some money saved up from my job back home, and I thought I could rent that Fiat I liked so much, at least for the first part..."

She trailed off when Sira's eyes joined her in smiling. "I think that sounds like a great idea. Where were you thinking of going?"

Little traced the explosion of lines on the paper, roads and rivers, all the paths that anybody could take, or not take. "Florence, I haven't been for years." Her finger began to trace downward as she continued, "And then Naples." She peeked over at her aunt. "To see Aunt Betty. I haven't seen her in years, either." *And maybe she'll tell me something useful,* she did not add. Sira raised a single eyebrow but did not object. Then she raised a finger to a point on the map just above Rome.

"You like fairy tales, so go over to Villa Gregoriana in Tivoli. It's only twenty minutes outside Rome. And Hadrian's Villa, you won't want to miss that, little ruin-chaser."

Sira seemed wary but not angry, though Little assumed she knew she would go to Betty to ask questions, and Little felt immeasurably relieved

"Do you think that it'll help? I want to know where I belong. Or, not just where do *I* belong, but also, always seeing people coming and going, the push and pull they feel to be different places..." Little was gesticulating wildly, unable to secure the words or herself. Though this was a big reason she wanted to leave, it wasn't the only one.

"I wander so that I may recognize home," murmured Sira, and Little looked at her, surprised.

"Yes." Sira nodded. "Your grandmother used to say to me that truly powerful people are the ones who do not allow external forces to invade their senses when they have a task that they cannot afford to fail. So whatever distractions you face, however unsure you are, when something is in your heart, you do it. You don't look left, you don't look right. Forget the chatter in your head. Just do it. I spent too much of my life listening to people tell me that starting is half the battle. Reality is, you have to fight the whole damn battle."

"Haven't you ever been afraid of anything?"

"Of course." Sira's face twisted, briefly, into a small smile.

"Did you ever not do something? Because you were afraid?"

"There were lots of things I didn't do because I was afraid, some so small I didn't even notice until later. That's why I'm telling you it's important."

"When we were having olive ascolane in Trastevere you told me about your father moving the family to Narni. I don't remember that story. I know you've told me a lot about your youth, but there are a lot of things I don't remember." What she meant but didn't say out loud was that she hadn't been listening then, and she wanted to listen now.

Sira smiled. "Of course. Let's make dinner first; one does nothing properly on an empty stomach."

***

"Your great-grandfather on your grandmother's side was a *guardiacaccia*," Sira began. "How do I say this? He was the keeper of the forest, to ensure that nobody hunted when they weren't supposed to. You like that, don't you? So did he. When I see you scribbling, I know you must have gotten it from him. He had the most beautiful handwriting I've ever seen. It must have gotten to him, because it got so that he wrote everything down, all the time. My great-grandmother used to laugh and say that when she wanted him to be quiet, she took his pencil away. I kept one of his logbooks for years. I do wish we hadn't lost that one in the move—one of the moves. It was one of the things I never wanted to lose, but there it is. Restarting does that, I suppose. His calligraphy was exquisite. Did you inherit that as well, Little? Let me see. Ah yes. Maybe just the love of writing, then…

"Your grandmother, his daughter, was a translator. She spoke Italian, French, and German. This saved us during the war, but it also made it so that we were always scared for her, every minute. When I was a girl, I thought this was how love always was, fraught with anxiety bordering on terror. Of course, that's a whole new word now, isn't it? For me, terror has always been a cold sweat. Just one feeling, rising up past your throat. In today's world, the word terror has taken on an even more dangerous nuance; it means misunderstanding, hatred breeding contempt, and then here we are, burning holes, destroying lifelines and ages and futures. But you're right, Little, I'm sorry. We're not talking about that today.

We were talking about my mother, and her languages. Once the Nazis figured out they could use her for her words, they liked her. This made it impossible for us to be invisible, which is the best thing to be during a war. They used to take her for days at a time, and every time, I thought, that's it. She's never coming back. But she always did, one way or the other. Once we had moved to Narni, she'd hitch rides on the German trucks going back to Rome so that she could take food to your grandfather. She hated them, but she needed them. I think we all felt that way. My blood runs cold at the thought of what could have happened. We're all much wiser in hindsight, aren't we? Was it so important to get him a home-cooked meal? I didn't understand it back then like I understand it now. Of course it was.

"You think you know love, Little? I hope for you that you do, that you will always feel that you know love more than any other feeling in the world, and that you feel less the lingering afterward when it hasn't gone right. My parents loved each other in a way that I have never seen since then. He used to brush her hair for her at night, just for the luxury of touching her. And when he had to, he kept himself apart from her, to keep her safe. He stayed behind in Rome during the war to work, but he sent us all to Umbria to be safe. To live in the country, where there is no war, he said. He was lying. War gets everywhere.

"But still, Narni it was. One afternoon I was in the yard that stretched down to the path when I saw a shape I couldn't make sense of. Mother ran out and grabbed me, squinting, and then began laughing. It was your grandfather, on a donkey. It was the only thing he could find to get him to the countryside to see us. Such a big man on such a little donkey. He had to keep his feet hitched up so that they wouldn't brush against the ground. I still laugh when I think about it. Mother cried. I didn't understand that then, either.

"I remember a day when we were still in Rome, when mother went to wait in line for food. We had rations. She waited hours and came home in tears because all that they had left was a carrot. You've heard worse stories than this, haven't you? Considering what some people went through, we really didn't have it so bad after all. This is nothing. Our story is a victory because we are still here to tell it. But the frustration, Little. That's what picks at you. That's what I remember the most, mother coming home to three kids with one carrot. She didn't even say anything, the tears just started. Like I told you, your father started coming home with food that he stole from the Nazi trucks. That scared my mother. We left Rome after that. The frustration, the total helplessness that begins to taste an awful lot like despair after too long. That's what you remember when it's over. It does different things to different people, those oily types of feelings.

"Once, two Greek soldiers came to our back door in Narni. They had deserted, I could smell it on them. Mother was horrified, but papà fed them and let them sleep in the barn before they went on their way. When mother told him he would get us all killed, killed I tell you, he looked at her quietly and told her, '*Chiunque ha paura ha diritto ad essere protetto.*' *Whoever is afraid has the right to be protected.*

"Can you look at someone quietly, Little? If anybody was capable of it, it was your grandfather. There was never anything loud in any of the ways that he moved, or spoke, or made decisions. But you never got the idea that you could forget any of those things.

"One of the men in town raised carrier pigeons. I like the Italian words for this better. *Piccioni viaggiatori.* Traveler pigeons. It sounds much braver, no? He raised them and trained them because they were sometimes used in the war effort to send messages. Little pigeons with messages tied to their feet, carrying state secrets. Except this man's didn't, because his pigeons always disappeared. They'd fly out, and many of them wouldn't come back. Do you want to know why? I used to kill them. Don't look so shocked. When mother was gone, she would leave one of the town girls to come over and take care of us, which was funny, because that girl needed more taking care of than we did. I made food, and we had no meat. My brother and sister were hungry, and I didn't want my brother stealing. I used to open the top window of the house, and the pigeons would be there, on the ledge, cooing. I don't know how I even thought of it. They weren't scared of me. I would stand there for a while so that they would get used to me, and then my hands would whip out ever so quickly and I'd break their necks. Then I would clean and roast them, and we would eat. In my whole life, I think that's the thing I feel the worst about. I don't recognize myself in those movements. But we needed meat, Little, do you understand that? I'm still sorry for it. Nobody ever found out. I never told. Nobody asked where the meat came from, but I did notice that nobody ever shrunk away from eating, either.

"Do you want to hear such things? I never knew how Italy was going to fight in the war. That's what made it so strange. We've never even been quite sure of ourselves. How were we going to present a united front? I look at my country today and I see something similar, and that frustration wells up again. Because my country today still doesn't know how to fight. Sure, it's a different confrontation. But it still doesn't know how to make decisions for the sake of its children. But those are my thoughts today. I was a little girl then, and those were not my thoughts.

"I learned during those days how to keep my mind from thinking of something on a loop by doing something else. I was a tiny little girl during the war, you know. Once mother didn't come back for three days. Is it cliché to say that it felt like an eternity? So I taught myself to make bread. I got so good at making bread that the neighbors' wives used to come over and ask if I would give them a loaf. I was so small I couldn't reach the top of the stove, so I would drag a stool and stand on top of it and make the best bread for miles around. I did it to keep my hands from shaking.

"It wasn't all bad. It almost never is, you know. When it was cold, we would light fires in the fireplace with dynamite we had stolen and make bruschetta. It was beautiful, the dynamite. You'd put the bread on the border of the fireplace with a little olive oil poured on top; yes, of course extra virgin, is there any other kind? I'm going to pretend you didn't even ask that. If we had tomatoes we would dice them and put them on top, and then slather it all in garlic. Wartime Italy. I can still smell the garlic.

"Rural Italy was… well, to be fair, if you go to some places now they will still make you feel the same way as they used to make us feel back then. Some of Italy feels frozen in time, like it had peeked into the future and decided, ah, better not. But the cities, the cities are different worlds now. Rome was so grand and majestic back then, like she still remembered where she came from, that she birthed the Caesars and the population that had owned the world. The Nazis were in awe of Rome, wanted to own it. Nobody owns Rome except for her people. You remember that, Little. Don't look at me like that. I know you think Rome royal, even now. I know how proud you are. It makes me glad. Your father would have been happy to see you look like that. He was the exact same way. I'm happy that makes you smile. But oh, I wish you could have seen her then. Rome at times reminds me of what I imagine it must feel like to be a very beautiful, aging woman, showing herself off—she reacquaints herself to you again in little pieces. Every time you're dazzled by a younger, more modern city, with its glitz and shine, Rome bides her time, and then she plays her cards. I have yet to see another city play a better hand.

"But enough about the war. What happened after? Well, I married the wrong man, of course. But that's another story, for another time.

"Do try not to be gone *too* long this trip, all right?"

***

And so it happened that two days later, Little found herself once again in the courtyard of her apartment complex in that early morning light that is scrubbed clean from a previous night's rain, worn map in hand. The car had a GPS, of course, rendering the map unnecessary, but Little held it lightly in her hand nonetheless, sure somehow that she would need it. She adjusted the uncomfortable straps of her backpack to keep them from chafing on her bare skin, waved once again to Sira, who stood in the window trying to be nonchalant, and turned toward the street that would take her to Termini station.

Once out on the street, she looked up and up at the silvery blue sky and whispered—to nobody, really—"Grant me eyes to see as though they have not seen before, a clean slate."

Little was on her way.

TRAVELS THROUGHOUT

Chapter 14
Tivoli, Italy. Present day.

Little began her adventures, for adventures is how she was beginning to think of them, by way of the Sabine town of Tivoli. She stopped to hike the park that was Villa Gregoriana, learning firsthand how apt her aunt had been when she deemed it a fairy tale. She was soon glad that she had worn her sneakers, as the expanse of land was, in actuality, a bubble of another world, and it is always best to have on proper shoes for other worlds. The canyon was a wood, and within it she found herself walking through rampant ruins of an ancient Roman villa, scrunching down to fit through secret tunnels and then, at the other end, stretching out to look for the waterfalls. *How lovely to be an element here*, she thought as the wind carried a tiny spray from the waterfalls above her. She could be anything at all that she wanted to be in this place, air or water or even earth, although probably not fire, she decided, looking around at all that grew around her.

I must remember all of this, she told herself. She felt an almost-forgotten, finger-tingling, chest-filling urge to write something down. Her fingers danced on the entrance to the second stone cave, and then through the grotto she found herself at the water's source, a bed of the Aniene River. Looking up, up, up at the leafy trees and silver-backed plants that seemed to have peaceably grown over everything, and with the thrum of the falls in her ears, she could see in the distance above her head the temples at the edge of the canyon, the ones in honor of, according to the nice guide she had encountered on the way in, mysterious deities.

"They could be to Vesta, the virgin goddess, or to Hercules, who protected the Tibur, or to the Tiburtine Sibyl," he had exclaimed gaily, one chubby finger pointing toward the two white structures on the other side of the water. "Best if you decide for yourself."

The ancient villa and gardens of the Emperor Hadrian, known in Italian as Villa Adriana, took her longer to reach than she had thought, mostly because she got herself thoroughly lost. Hadrian's retreat from the city he had ruled for a time was vast, dotted with ruins and pools— no fools, the ancient emperors—and alternated between haunting and enchanting, with gnarled trees growing over the landscape and a lost temple at seemingly every turn. Little, looking at one such veneration, wondered what it must feel like to be a forgotten god.

She busied herself climbing around the ancient structures, trying to be as respectful as it is possible to be in the house of the old while also sweating profusely under a lion sun. Since there weren't many visitors to the grounds, it was easy enough for her to pretend that she was an ancient warrior out finding her luck, seeing as she did not so much fancy the idea of being the woman who waited at home for the aforementioned warrior. When the crooked road before her opened up to a wide pathway lined with cypresses, she decided to be an ancient Roman goddess. Did the Romans have a god of time? They should, she considered, looking around in what she was certain was a grand manner, because somebody needed to keep track of it around these parts.

There seemed to be gods for most anything, she mused. Noticing the plants that grew over one of the pools that still held water, Little imagined what the villa must have looked like at the height of its splendor. It would have been regal, must have felt impervious to time. Anyone walking through its grounds then would never imagine that it would one day, centuries later, lie desolate yet still be standing, that later generations would walk past the water and the shrubs of rosemary still scenting the air and wonder about what had come before them. She fantasized that the earth might shake, the gods warning of the passage of time. She raised her arms over her head, lost in the moment, sunlight flickering through her fingers as she raised her head. She thought she could hear bellowing in the distance, ghosts walking the halls of their ancient home, with the sky and the sun as its roof.

"Hello," said a voice behind her.

Little jumped and twisted around to face the voice. A tall young man, with curly dark hair and eyes of a matching color, was watching her curiously. Little suddenly became aware that she had come to the end of the path, and was standing at the edge of the pool, holding a sprig of rosemary in the air. She dropped it and hoped quite fervently that he had not caught the moment when she had been talking to time past with athletic hand gestures.

"Hello," she said back, squinting as she looked up. He looked about her age.

"I was wondering if you knew where the exit is. I'm afraid I'm lost. I'm so relieved you speak English," the man said. Little blinked and realized that, yes, they were indeed speaking English. He thrust out his hand, and Little took it.

"I'm David. Visiting here with my family. We're from the States."

David, and not the diminutive, she noticed. Little appreciated people who took their given names seriously.

"Little. I live here."

"Cool name. What were you doing just then? Before?" He had a lovely smile.

I was impersonating a goddess, and if you had been quiet a little longer, I would undoubtedly have embarrassed myself even more thoroughly by beginning to talk right out loud.

"I was, uh, I'm practicing for a play. The exit is this way, by the way. I walked by it before. I'll show you. Are you meeting your family there?"

"I am. We were all walking together, but I got lost." He blushed slightly. "I wandered off, actually. It's just so beautiful here, like you could be anything, see anything. I got so caught up watching everything that was going on above my head and below my feet that next thing you know, I was standing next to the statue and found you with your arms flung open, holding a plant. It took me a second to realize you were real." He looked down and smiled at her, and this time it was her turn to blush. "So you're from here?" he continued, and she nodded.

"Yep. I grew up in California, though," she clarified as they halted to let a group of tourists walk ahead of them. David looked after them with an air of curiosity.

"You know what," he said once they had passed, "there's a different air over here, somehow. Everyone I meet here looks like they're coming *from* someplace, whereas back home everyone seems to be going *to* someplace. Do you think that's an Italy thing?" He looked at her inquisitively.

"I don't know," she replied honestly. Then, "Can't one have both? A place to be from, and a place to go to?"

He smiled appreciatively. "I hope so."

The conversation flowed easily during the stroll toward the main exit, and speaking in English with someone whose verbal cadence was so familiar made Little terribly and unexpectedly homesick.

"So where are you from?" she asked him as they picked their way slowly through the paths.

"Washington, DC, but I'm going to school in Colorado."

"I love Colorado," Little answered, "except for the cold winters."

"Spoken like a true Californian!" He looked down at her and grinned. "Funny, to talk about those places here, huh? It feels like we're talking about someplace not real, but that we both somehow know about."

Little felt the very real tug of the San Francisco Bay pulling at her. "Maybe," she ventured, "you feel that way because you know you're going back," then immediately felt silly. *Why am I always looping back to this? Can't I have a normal conversation?* She chided herself angrily, looking up at the handsome boy with the tousled hair.

"Maybe that's why. You're not?"

"No. Not right now. So, what's DC like?" she asked, hoping to distract him, and although his glance belied he'd noticed, he let her change the subject and gladly told her about his home city. The fact that David knew her home made her feel so familiar that for a moment, she forgot where she was. By the time they had found his family she desperately wanted to cling to them and ask if they might take her in, she wouldn't be too much of a bother, and they could take her on the plane as carry-on baggage. Instead, she smiled and waved, trying hard not to cry, while the friendly group of sunburned, tall American tourists departed. She felt blindsided by the feeling of swirling water in the pit of her stomach, and suddenly felt stupid and embarrassed with herself at having spent so much of her day prancing about pretending to be something she was certainly not. She pulled out her car keys and decided to go into town and find a place to sleep for the night. She conceded herself a small sniffle.

***

The twisting roads on the way back to town had eventually led to a colorful main street brimming with tiny local shops all in the busy process of shutting down for the night. She had walked into one and asked if they might recommend a place to sleep, and the shop owners had cheerfully pointed her just down the road to a little bed-and-breakfast. While being shown her room, she had noticed a miniature bookcase crammed with treasures, she imagined, left behind by previous guests. The proprietress, having noticed her long glance, had smiled and said that she was more than welcome to pick out a book to take with her. Little had answered politely that she had brought some books with her, but that she might have a look later.

She couldn't sleep. She had decided where she would go next, so that wasn't what was keeping her up. Rome was keeping her up, the city insinuating itself in her veins and settling there in a way she had avoided for two years. Now, staring up at the ceiling, she searched for distractions. A quick glance at the desk by her bed registered the two books she had brought with her—one that she was halfway finished with and had adored so far, and one a novel she had picked up on recommendation of a friend but which she had found difficult to lose herself in. She opened the small orange volume to her bookmark, a miniature magnetic flip-flop that pointed to where she had last given up, about fifty pages in. Then, remembering the bookcase, she set the book down and hauled herself out of bed.

Meandering down the quiet hallway, she peeked out the windows at the dark sky and saw that the property boasted a sprawling garden, just haphazard enough to be pleasantly friendly and sprinkled with small lights. Maybe the owners wouldn't mind if she sat outside for a while. She reached the little bookcase, about half her height, and crouched down to skim through the titles. About halfway through she found a mid-sized book with a deep blue cover on which was etched a dragonfly, the creature's delicate tail serving as the first letter of the book's title. She read the back and gazed at the minute gold animal for a few moments before getting up, running back to her room, and grabbing the orange book from the table. *Sorry*, she mouthed as she removed her bookmark and walked back to the bookcase. "I'm sure you'll find someone who will appreciate you more than I have," she told it as she slid the other, well-worn book out, replacing it with the newness of the little volume. *There*, she thought. *A book for a book.*

She ventured down to the room that opened out into the garden, the dragonfly book in one hand. No one was there except for a small potted plant in the center of the room. Little had noticed, and appreciated, that all the plants and flowers she had seen here were alive and not cut, tucked into their own sturdy pots filled with rich earth. She moved past the door to the outside quietly, wondering if she was allowed, and sat on a carved bench. There was that feeling in her fingers again, the one she had felt in Tivoli, when she had been buoyed by the wind that flew through the park and danced with the cold, clear water of the falls that fed the canyon. An image flashed in her mind of Sira, reaching out to pick her wayward scarf out of the sky, taking it from the breeze to settle it once more around her neck. The elements, she had said, are not in my favor today. "It's a child's urge," she said to a waving oak that grew next to the bench, "and I'm grown up now. There's no room for stories." For a few moments she gazed, unfocused, into the leaves of the trees. Then she sighed, stood up, and headed back to her room, where she knew she would find paper and a pencil.

The Elements

The elements live in Rome, or rather, they always come back to her. Air loves to whistle around the mighty structure rebuilt by Hadrian but bearing the name of Agrippa, whose name is inscribed on its portico and with which he achieved immortality rather more easily than some of his fellow Roman statesmen. Roaring over the oculus of this Pantheon, designed to revere the gods of the planets and welcome the rain, Air jumps to the nooks and crannies of Piazza Navona, delighted that it has not changed in what to men are thousands of years and to Air is a mere flurry. After all, she needs nothing to survive, generating her own energy, which others sometimes harness. She much prefers to be referred to as Wind, fancying herself more active than the other elements give her credit for. You would think, she likes to mention, that at least Fire would support her, seeing as she feeds him. But Fire insists on calling her nothing at all, resentful as he is that he is nothing when she lacks; in truth, he hates her more than he hates Water, who at least is open in her disdain of him.

Earth never leaves, but that is because Earth is always present, so it really isn't showing much of a preference that way. Still, Earth has largely left Rome to it, trying not to shake too hard for fear of bringing down the Colosseo, which it is particularly fond of. It knows that the structure was built to stand against its quakes but no longer would, thanks to the thieves of the Renaissance period. It shivered in protest during those times, but now holds still. There are the volcanoes anyway, for when

Earth can't hold it in anymore. Earth does not have a gender, so it finds it much easier to get along than its three counterparts, who are defined by theirs. Aether, filling the sky, is also above mere gender, but they never talk about it. Aether, as a rule, considers itself above the basic elements. Earth grumbles, but not too loudly.

Fire most enjoys Campo de' Fiori, where he burned Giordano Bruno at the stake hundreds of years ago for daring to suggest that the universe is infinite. He still plays around the edges of the piazza, where the morning market and evening antics provide more than enough chaos to keep him fed and fat. Still, of all the elements Fire finds the least reign in Rome, although in days of old he burned in the soul of the Senate itself. Today Fire takes his glory from his city just after dawn and just before dusk, burnishing everything with his brush of vermilion, the color that scoops under the pines and dances across the ocher walls of Roman homes, setting them alight. This is the most Fire can take today; this he blames on Water.

Water is by far the favored element of the city of Rome, and she returns gladly, endlessly surprised by the city's changes as well as its ability to remain exactly the same. Holding her breath, Water pours through the aqueducts built in her honor and flows out through the fountains without discriminating against the famous public *nasoni*, where people and animals drink freely, and the timeless fountains that mark the city's history, from the Trevi to the Barcaccia of Piazza di Spagna. If she has to choose, she does not love Trevi the most, as it is riotous and people insist on throwing coins inside; she much prefers to rush over the cobblestones, endlessly in pursuit of the cats of the city, although she well knows that Rome is owned by these felines and she would do best not to anger them. Still, she knows she is also a force to be reckoned with here, that the Romans revere her so deeply that they will stop everything when she patters over them.

The elements often live in Rome, although she is not their sole motivation: Air, Water, and Earth often enjoy that ode to the natural forces, Villa Gregoriana in nearby Tivoli. (Fire is, once again, asked to kindly keep out.) Air whistles down through the canyon, Water finds herself once again in its many waterfalls, and Earth burrows down through the ancient excavated ruins. The temples are in their honor, they are certain. And when they are done, there are endless more treasures to be discovered. The elements know this well, and so they are gentle with Rome; after all, she has already withstood much, and they do so love to take rest within her walls.

And so Rome feeds the elements, and in return, they keep her safe.

Chapter 15
Rome. 1995.

Enrico leaned heavily against the bar, looking around himself in the almost empty room. He stood almost a head above the few other people scattered about the café, so he didn't have to meet anyone's eye. As he scanned the back of the room, the door chimed and his sister walked in.

"*Sorella mia,*" he said, rising to greet her. She lashed him a smile.

"You must need something, *fratello*, if we're already talking about our blood ties." She kissed him on each cheek to put him at ease and settled herself in the seat next to his. "Is this about that abominable spectacle last week? I certainly hope not," she said as she unwrapped the dark green scarf from around her neck and placed it on the back of her chair, "though I admit I've been wondering how you're planning on handling this one. And why you've disappeared since then." She sat back and looked at Enrico squarely.

"It's not going to work."

"What? Your sham of a marriage?"

Enrico flinched. "Sometimes I wish you weren't quite so harsh."

Sira waved her hand in the air in a dismissive gesture. "And I adore you, but sometimes I wish you weren't such an ostrich. We all have our burdens to bear."

"Can you take her?" Enrico asked, dropping his voice and his eyes.

Sira froze. "Enrico, I know the situation is very distressing, but surely…"

"So you already know what I'm asking."

"I think I do, yes. And I don't want you to think that I don't want to help, but Delila already seems to be under the impression that I'm in the way. Though I do think you should make frighteningly certain that woman knows that if she ever lays a finger on my niece again, as sorry as I might feel for Delila's situation, I will rip her fingernails out."

"It's temporary. It's only temporary, we only need a little time and then Little can come back."

"But surely Little isn't the problem?"

There was something he did not want to tell her, she could tell by the way his eyes flickered around the room, unwilling to rest on her face; by the way he was twisting his fingers.

"Of course not. You're the international one, Sira. The adventurous one. I know you can take care of her. And you've wanted to go back to California. Take her away from this messy situation so that I can deal with it without harming my daughter. Please. I don't want her to pay the price." His mouth grimaced involuntarily, and Sira reached out instinctively before realizing she did not know what to do. Enrico finally looked his sister in the eye, dark mahogany meeting brilliant green. "She's hit her since then."

Sira felt the room slow, the air around her harden. Her breath caught as she controlled a sweep of rage. "What?"

"Yes," Enrico's voice pitched lower, his hands ensnared in each other. "I don't know what to do. I don't know what to do. Any excuse seems good enough. As soon as Little does anything Delila doesn't like, she gets a slap. She's never been hit in her life, Sira. No one's ever touched her that way. She comes crying to me, and I don't know what to do. Delila is angry. She's angry, and she has every right to be. But her anger should be for me. I can't stand it if she hits Little again, I can't stand it. My child cannot have bruises." His hands entwined themselves in his hair and he leaned over in his seat as though he would vomit. Sira rather thought she might, too. "It's my fault," Enrico whispered to the tabletop. Sira straightened her back.

"Regardless of whose fault it is, Enrico, and under no circumstances do I think you're an innocent in all of this, I think you need to put that aside and think of your daughter's best interest first. I see your reasoning now. I'll take Little. But I'll take her now, Enrico. We'll leave tomorrow." Sira tried to keep her voice steady. Enrico looked up at her.

"Only for a time, Sira. We need some time, Delila and I, to figure things out, and then I'll come and bring Little back."

"Fratello, I do not wish to add to your burdens, but listen to me very carefully. I have tried not to over-involve myself in your life, or in your decisions. I've backed you up, and I will continue doing so. You are my family. You are my only brother. But let me be clear, because more important things are at stake here than the family you've been trying to build with the wrong pieces: I will let Delila in the same house as Little only when I am convinced beyond any reasonable doubt that she would never lay a finger on her child again, and that would take a lot of convincing."

Enrico shook his head slightly. "This isn't going to be an issue, Sira. Everything is going to work out fine. I'm going to handle this situation."

"Alright," she said, wanting to believe him.

"You'll never tell her?"

"What?"

"Never tell Little how her father ruined everything?"

"You can't *do* that to your child, Enrico," Sira said, throwing her hands up as the frustration and sensation of helplessness finally got the best of her.

"It doesn't change anything for her. It keeps her safe and happy. Why does it matter? I want my daughter to love me."

"Why wouldn't she love you, anyway? There will come a time when she will have to know things for how they really went. Otherwise you'll be taking away her right to *decide* whether it matters or not!" *You're taking it away out of fear that it will ruin her image of you, and that's selfish,* she thought, but she knew she would have to be careful how she phrased herself. "You have memories, and Delila has memories, and even tiny Little has already begun to have memories. And the sum of all those still does not make the truth. Remember where it's gotten you so far, Enrico. You and that father of Delila's. Not telling the truth warps the other person's ability to make decisions. Surely you've learned that by now?"

Enrico shook his head, annoyed. "I really don't see how that's relevant. It's simply not important. She will not form a concept of herself based on this, she'll build it through her own experiences. These days will be nothing but a wisp of a memory, and it can be buried under better, happier times."

Sira looked back at him with her level, steady gaze. "You're right, I certainly hope that these days will be forgotten," she shook her head slightly at Enrico's brightening expression, to signal that she hadn't yet finished her thought—her brother always took what he wanted to hear from a phrase—"but by concealing it when she's older, you will make it important to her down the line. And then maybe it *will* shape her. Aren't we also the sum of the people who have loved us? And I'm sure you're right, and she won't shape a concept of herself on one thing alone. But be careful, fratello mio. If you keep this from her, it may define her concept of *you*."

At this, Enrico's expression shuttered, and he turned his face away from hers. She waited patiently while he looked across the room at the mirror under the bar, all dark eyes and stubborn expression. He wasn't studying himself; she sometimes thought his stoic good looks were something he barely registered. Instead, he was looking at her in the mirror thoughtfully. She raised her eyebrows slightly and looked down at the drink the waiter had brought her before they had begun their conversation, the cold smell of the alcohol in her cup reaching up to wrinkle her nose. She pushed it away. She didn't like drinking anyway, had only ordered an alcoholic drink because the mysterious atmosphere of the café seemed to require it. *How silly of me*, she thought, raising her hand to catch the waiter's attention and ask him for an *espresso doppio*. Enrico finally turned back toward her. Sira kept her eyes focused on the waiter's back.

"You'll take her?" he repeated. His expression was pained.

"You know that I will. You know how I love the child. I would do this for you even if I didn't love her, but as it is, for me it is as though she were my own."

Enrico's lips turned down slightly at the corners. "You shouldn't let Anna hear you say that."

This time it was Sira's turn to be surprised.

"Surely it's not a competition. And Anna is a grown woman. Little is a child."

Enrico raised his eyebrows. "Yes, and love isn't a thing that people compete over, right?" he said slowly.

"Ah yes," Sira said in a curt tone, "please do tell me about the best way to raise a child."

"You won't tell Little?"

Sira paused.

"You won't tell her?" he repeated quietly, holding his sister's green gaze. "I will handle this situation," he promised vehemently.

"Which part am I not to tell her? About this issue with Delila, or about the things you and Beppe Selinti kept from her that put you all in this situation?"

Enrico shook his head. "Please, Sira, I'm tired. I'm tired and I want to focus on moving *forward*."

"Alright," she conceded slowly, "I won't speak a word of it. You're her father, and it will be up to you. But be careful, Enrico. I am worried about where this will go, not just for Little, but also for you." She reached a hand out to him. "You are not as tough as you like to think you are. But you are a grown man, and I won't try to baby you. But step with care, brother of mine. Make sure that this situation doesn't handle *you*. Remember what mamma used to say to us, about broken things. They always break along the same lines. I don't want that for you, Enrico. You have to look at the truth."

Enrico reached for the jacket he had thrown haphazardly over the chair next to him. "This is my family, Sira, not a vase. Everything will work itself out," he said as he rose, though his confidence was still missing. "Little will be safe, and once I've worked this out with Delila we'll be a real family again. Little will never have to deal with this. It will never matter again."

"I hope you're right," Sira said, swallowing the last words that she had been about to say: I hope Little doesn't have to pay for it when it turns out it does matter.

Chapter 16
Florence, Italy. Present day.

Florence was a city so beautiful it took Little's breath away. She was staying at an *agriturismo*, the Italian version of a bed-and-breakfast, half an hour outside of the city. Renting a car, it turned out, was a mite more expensive than she had foreseen, and so she had returned her loyal 500 to the car company at the airport, patting its hood in thanks as she walked out of the parking lot. She was relying on trains and buses to move about now and tried to convince herself that this would be more interesting, anyway. She missed the car's air-conditioning after about five minutes of the train's faulty air system, but with the train itself having been half an hour late, she supposed she should be thankful she was on it at all.

The Florentine couple that owned the agriturismo were soft-spoken, and their walls were filled with art, beautiful pieces both collected and created by themselves and the families that had raised them. They were writers and artists, and they both loved their city and respected her. Once they heard Little did not know Florence well, they were happy to take her under their wing, proudly showing her their city. Marta and Rolando ferried her back and forth from their little residence, sitting companionably with her on the train. In the evenings, they would take the same train back to the little town, and here, Little felt, was *la Toscana* in all of its real glory. They ate food so fresh she became endlessly grateful for the existence of taste buds. Although she was their only guest, they would insist on cooking full meals at dinnertime, colorful plates laid out on the front porch, with a neighbor oftentimes dropping in for company.

Like many agriturismi, the house produced its own olive oil and wine; also like many others, they risked having to close. They discussed it in earnest one evening, and Little was reminded of hushed conversations overheard on the buses, in restaurants, and from her own family growing up. For the first time, though, she did not feel disconnected from it, as though it were all happening somewhere else, to someone else, and she leaned in closer to hear Marta speak. Marta always wore cotton dresses and sensible hiking boots, her dark hair pulled back, eyes slightly slanted against high cheekbones. Little found her riotously beautiful.

"We're selling an original product—" she gestured to the verdant olive oil that Little had been dipping her bread in for the past half hour, a process the Italians called *inzuppare*—"but we cannot cut costs as much as the bigger houses, and so cheaper olive oil is what makes it over the sea. I'll take you to see the olive tree grove before you leave, Little…"

Little developed the habit of going to bed early, retiring to her little room with its clean cotton sheets and writing more than she had in years, one ear tuned in to the cicadas buzzing outside while she went through sheaf after sheaf of paper as stories roiled around, absorbing Marta's softer words and Rolando's insistence on updating her on the current political situation, on little Italy in-between, as he put it. Later, in the quiet safety of her room, she slept like the number four, with one leg tucked up securely behind the gentle slope of the back of her knee, and the music of the serenading insects slipped into her dreams. When she woke up one morning, she wrote down the dream that had filled her sleep, one of tiny creatures and those still willing to listen to their music. A big believer in naming things, she scribbled a title across the top of the page before running out to meet Marta: What Sings in the Night.

Having been raised hiking Mount Tamalpais, she quickly took to countryside walks with Marta, thrilled when she pointed out the forest animals that dozed in the day or chittered up above their heads. Ambling through the trees reminded her of the long walks she had taken when she had been in Sperlonga as a teenager, those months where she had felt forlorn and forgotten. But now she did not feel alone, and wandering felt not like a search but a destination in itself. She was delighted when she discovered that mushroom picking was actually something people did in real life and not just in fairy tales. Later, tasting Marta's *tagliatelle ai funghi porcini*, she was forced to amend that thought; this was, must be, a fairy tale.

The three of them walked through Florence, with Rolando, jovial and pot-bellied, reciting his favorite passages from Dante Alighieri. Little found herself hoping that the city could hear their ode, a celebration to the birth of the modern Italian language that had once taken place in this very city. They took Little to all the places they loved, the *David* and the crowded Uffizi but also the markets, the shops of the artisans, and the leather school, where Little found a pocket-sized notebook of deep red leather with a sash to tie it. Rolando spotted her holding it in her hand and insisted, with a flourish, on buying it for her.

"But Rolando, it's not necessary!" she had laughed when he had ceremoniously presented it to her, and he had thrown his head back in mock seriousness. "A gift for you to remember another valiant city, little Roman!" He slid his hand into the crook of Marta's elbow and waltzed her into the street.

When Little noticed how many street artists there were, Rolando's eyes lit up and, speaking to both his wife and his young guest, asked, "If the rain washes away the drawings of a Florentine street artist, did they ever exist?"

"Definitely. Yes," answered Little, watching the rivulets of color as they melted into the concrete. She felt Rolando and Marta's approval warm her shoulders.

Then a day dawned, and Little, following the cadence her travels seemed to be taking, knew it was time for her to go, though she thought she would maybe stay forever if she could. That was the day that Marta and Rolando took her to see their olive grove, and standing on the edge of their lands, they held hands and looked out over their bent, sturdy trees and rolling hills, eyes flashing with mixed helplessness and a refusal to give in to the odds mounting against them. On the walk back to the tawny building that perched on the edge of their property, diminutive Marta, who had no children of her own, hooked her arm through Little's, and Little felt a warm surge inside her heart.

What Sings in the Night

Tok tok. Ahem. Is everyone ready? Now, it's such a velvet evening that I think we can really count on admirable acoustics. I want a top-notch performance. Woodwinds! Bass! Percussion! Strings! Have you practiced?

Cicadas in the trees, step forward, if you please. A nice loud zing. Yes, just like that! Crickets? Can we have a trill and a chirp? Perfect. Everyone, please base yourselves on this. Frogs and toads, line up your lily pads! You are instruments of this forest orchestra as well, you know. We'll need a good, deep vibration from the pond if we are to have a decent symphony; I want to hear it all the way through the blades of grass on the other side.

Grasshoppers, unite! You are keeping time tonight. Balance, *per favore*. We're all relying on you.

Alright. Owls, with your mighty wings and lonely eyes, we're ready! Chorus!

Bullfrog, tiny and squat, are you hiding? It's your turn! And you thought a car could roar!

Where are the katydids? This won't work without them! The moon has moved enough in the sky, so it is your turn, you who look most like the leaves. Sing the songs you were named for, for if we cannot see you then we must know you by your call: kai-tee-did, kai-tee-did!

All together now, so that the woodland echoes! Closest to the dawn the chirping birds will take over, but right now, now is the hour of us, the little beings. After all, we've lived in tandem with the humans all these long years, and while their empires rise and fall, we make our music.

What do you mean, I'm just a field mouse with a stick and nobody will hear us anyhow? *This is a baton.* Why, my mighty family has conducted this orchestra for uncountable decades, and you will refer to me as Maestro, if you please! Take it from the top—give them something to remember!

We may be background noise; but then again, there are always those who listen.

Chapter 17
Naples, Italy. Present day.

Aunt Betty was not technically anybody's aunt, but she had been Sira's best friend in California for many years before Little's birth, and Little had always considered the tall, gregarious woman a part of her own little family. Betty was voluptuous, blonde, and blue-eyed, the antithesis of Sira in almost every physical way. They shared the same wry sense of humor and innate love of the world that circled them, and so had become fast friends since the day Betty, backing out of a parking spot, had almost run Sira down next to their local supermarket. Betty had a dancer's mind; she waltzed with her words, and when Little was still very small and fresh from Italy, Betty worried that she would not find herself in this big American world, shy as she was, and so she reveled in teaching Little the nuances of the English language. The first journal Little ever had was a gift from Betty, and Little was enthralled by the sheer possibility of it. Betty nurtured the little girl's innate love for books and literature, showed her that it was impossible to be lonely if one had a book nearby, or pen and paper. Because of this, Little was one of the only students in her class who did not dread summer reading assignments or book fairs, and instead would run home with lists of titles in her hands, bursting through the door to ask Sira if they could please go to the library, yes, right now, and Sira and Betty always complied.

Betty had thought that, if given a safe place to retreat and a mastery of the language that was not her first, the girl would venture out and make her own friends without feeling as though she were somehow inferior.

She was gratified when she saw that this is what happened, and though Little had been too young then to have actively realized what Betty had conspired to do for her, she had grown up adoring the boisterous woman who was only too happy to whisk seven-year-old Little away for a drive over to Tiburon to have an ice cream at the unheard-of hour of nine in the evening.

On one of her trips to Italy with Sira and her little niece, Betty had met Alessandro, a broad-shouldered Napoletano with a husky laugh, and had promptly married him and moved to Naples without so much as a backward glance for her adopted state of California or her home city of Chicago. Little had thought she was very brave. Sira had thought she was crazy. Regardless, Betty had been living with Alessandro in Naples for well over ten years now, and Little, who hadn't seen her in many years, was excited to see a friendly face among all the strange things happening to her lately.

As the train pulled into the station of Napoli Centrale, Little had no trouble picking out the tall, straight-backed form of Betty, who tended to be quite a bit taller than the Italians, and when the two locked eyes it was as though no time had passed at all. She grabbed her bag and flew off the train straight into Betty's outstretched arms.

"Look at you! You've turned into a woman! Oh, welcome back, my darling." Betty was crying, her slender hands on Little's face, and Little noted without quite meaning to that there was no judgment in Betty's voice. With a little lurch, the defensive walls that had felt as though they had grown permanently around her heart began to recede.

She hugged Betty hard. "You look amazing, Aunty Betty," she said. It was true: Betty tended to look as though she had not aged, and though she was well into her seventies by now, the only thing that gave her away were the fine webs that spread out from her eyes, the ones that crinkled when she laughed. They were quite deep, and Little reasoned that she probably laughed a lot.

"So do you, girl. Gosh, your eyes. You look just like him. I hope you don't think it's insensitive of me to say so." Betty had known Little's father for as many years as she had known Sira, and had been not-so-secretly taken with him for many years until she had met Alessandro.

134

Little, looking bashful, swung her bag over her shoulder as Betty squeezed her and they headed out of the station together.

"I thought we could spend a few days in the city to show you around, show you how pizza is really done," she said as they piled into her tiny baby blue car, one eyebrow raised to show what she thought of the thin-crusted Roman way of making pizza. "Then we can take you out to the country house a bit out of Naples, and you can meet Parnassius."

"What is a Parnassius?" Little asked, but Betty waved her away, threading into the chaotic traffic of the city. Little sat back, feeling the muscles in her lower back slowly start to unknot, and closed her eyes.

When Betty glanced over at her, Little's mouth was slightly open in sleep. Betty remembered the conversation she had had that morning with Sira, who was almost delirious with worry over the child, telling Betty in spurts that she was worried that Little would not adjust to life in Italy. California is so different, she had said, and Betty had laughed; we would know, my friend. *Not a child anymore, anyway*, Betty realized now, brushing back a stray lock of dyed blonde hair from the girl's forehead. At a red light, she noticed an open notebook spilling out of Little's backpack, and she tucked it back inside. As she did up the zip, she saw Little's handwriting scrawled across the page, and though she looked away, knowing Little would not want to be read without being asked, she smiled to herself.

***

In keeping with her nascent habit of anthropomorphizing her cities, Little decided that as a woman, Naples would be sharp-eyed and heavy-hipped, quick to anger but also to comfort, and that her life would have been one to make a lesser woman tremble. She would wear a riot of colors, and her features would be quick but defined, as though sculpted by a heavy hand that had lingered; her skirts would be voluminous, so as to shelter her loved ones; her shoes sensible, so that she could run from danger, as well as from the country that had created and subsequently shunned her. She would love music, and would have perfected the Italian *arte di arrangiarsi*, the art of making the best of things. Naples, Little thought, would be a shameless woman out of necessity, fiercely loyal and intense, a being who hid her rags behind the indigo and turquoise of her bay.

The first time she saw the Gulf of Naples, with Mount Vesuvius rising in the background like an unsettled monument, she confirmed her thoughts: Naples was a deity to be revered. *And worthy of being honored with more than the trash littered throughout the city*, she thought grimly, picking her way through what could only be described as filth.

Alessandro took her to explore the city—sometimes with Betty, sometimes just the two of them—while he told her about the water-born Naples he had grown up in. "This city has *brio*, Little," he'd say in his thick Neapolitan Italian, hands waving vigorously, and Little would think that he and Betty made a fantastic match. They ate the thick pizza that was typical of Napoli ("Typical?" he'd exclaimed when she made the mistake of using this word in front of him. "We are the masters of pizza, this is the home of pizza!"), and Alessandro taught Little bits and pieces of the dialect, showed her the chaotic pieces Caravaggio had left behind during his exile from Rome.

One day, he took her to the ludicrously beautiful, imperial Piazza del Plebiscito, set her with her back to the mighty Palazzo Reale, and pointed to the bronze horses ahead of her. "Now, you walk between them," he said, and she looked at him curiously. "With your eyes closed." She was surprised by the resistance in her legs and took longer than she'd imagined, and by the end they were both laughing uproariously. Alessandro finally pointed out the almost imperceptible slope of the piazza. "Harder than it looks," he said, "but if you try, you can do it." He'd patted her hand, and Little had known this was as close as he could get to being downright reassuring.

***

Near dawn one morning, when the city was still curled up in sleep, Betty took Little through the unusually quiet streets to the waterfront, stopping just before the curve into the waves. Putting her hands on

Little's shoulders, she pointed to the right, where a palace stood on the border between land and sea, melancholy, quietly crumbling away. Little's breath caught in her throat.

"That is Palazzo Donn'Anna. It was a wedding present from the Spanish viceroy of Naples to his love, Anna Carafa. He left her for Spain in the middle of the 17th century, and she died, brokenhearted, not long after that. The architect gave up on the project, and that was that. She sits here, desolate. But she is undeniable, is she not?" Betty had always had an eye for the tragically beautiful and deemed the Palazzo the summary of her chosen city. She had wanted Little to see it before she left.

They stood and listened to the waves, watching the endless sea for almost an hour before Betty steered Little away, assuming correctly that there is always an optimal time for coffee.

Curled up in a seaside café (bar, Little reminded herself), nursing Neapolitan coffee and a *sfogliatella* pastry, Betty fixed Little with the no-nonsense look she remembered from when she was seven and determined to convince Betty she had not, in any way, previously consumed ice cream that day, so please, could Betty buy her one?

"So. Sira's been telling you stories about your grandparents, huh?" she flicked a crumb from her chin and surveyed Little with some curiosity.

"Yes. Did she tell you that?"

"Mmmhmm," was Betty's noncommittal response. "What I want to know is, Little, has she told you anything about herself?"

"What do you mean?"

"About Sira. About her marriage, her back and forth. About the woman she was. Is."

Little frowned. "I know about the woman she is."

"No, you don't. I say this with love in my heart, but you're at an age where you think you invented everything you're going through now. Sira is a woman in her own right, and while I respect her privacy, I do think that it would help you to know that the things you are feeling, that you are contending with inside yourself, are similar in a lot of ways to what Sira went through. She went back and forth, too, Little, did you never think that? Did you think she was never torn between

Italy and the United States, between the people she loved that lived so many miles and hours apart? That she spent her life trying to force two countries physically closer, by sheer force of her will? It's a lot to take on, a whole continent."

"I never really got the idea that her husband was all that important to her, frankly," Little said with a shrug, and Betty grimaced and shook her head.

"She's not doing you any favors acting like none of it mattered, even though I understand what she's trying to do. She's trying to protect you from it. I think she hopes that if she doesn't tell you how intense things were for her sometimes, that somehow you won't have to go through it. I've always said this to her, and she's never listened: Feelings aren't viruses. She's not condemning you to anything by being honest. I think she's worried that somehow, because you were exposed to being in different places when you were very young, that you're forced into one set path of being wayward. Which, incidentally, is not always a bad thing. But you do know, Little, that you make your own choices, don't you?"

She leaned in to look at Little's dark brown eyes with her own clear blue ones; Little nodded, swallowed.

"Didn't you wonder why she didn't go back with you when you left Italy after Enrico died?" Betty asked, her tone softening.

Little cocked her head. "Actually, yes. But I never knew how to bring that up to her, not without sounding accusatory."

Betty nodded. "I think she finally needed to stake a claim on a home. And I do wonder if she feels that she wasn't mother enough to Anna when she was growing up. I wonder if she was hoping that staying in Italy this time would make up for the times when she hadn't. I've talked to Sira about the problem between you and Anna, you know. I've never known Anna well, but I get the feeling she has more of an issue with her mother than she does with you. I think her resentment of you has more to do with the fact that you stole her title as Sira's daughter, and her role as Enrico's."

"I *stole* it?"

"Well, that might be how I'd see it if I were her. You have all these years with Sira that she didn't have."

"But then couldn't I be resentful that she got all those years with my dad?" Little asked, remembering the conversation with Anna in Sperlonga, that feeling of being inadvertent parallels.

"Sure. Are you?"

Little looked down at her sfogliatella. "No," she decided, and Betty smiled.

"Good girl."

"Wouldn't it make more sense for us to be close because of all the things, people, we have in common?"

Betty sighed. "Introspection is a tough game, Little. I'd say that yes, you're completely right. But it's hard to be logical when there are years of emotions pushing their way into your thought processes. It takes a very... special kind of person to cut through resentment. It's a thick substance, and sometimes it's easier to just go with it."

"I'm not sure this whole being an adult thing is quite what it's cracked up to be," Little ventured, and Betty's eyes sparkled.

"It's a trick for sure. Don't do it if you can avoid it."

"Can you tell me? Can you tell me some things about Sira? Would that be alright?" Little asked, and Betty nodded.

"Yes. It would be. Because I told her I would tell you...

"I know you know the basics, the facts, the snippets that seem like they are all that's important. You know that Sira moved to California initially because she fell in love with an American, that she married and had Anna there. You know that the marriage fell apart, that she took her daughter back to Italy, and that Anna then wanted to stay in Italy with Enrico, even though Sira wanted to go back to California. The similarities, huh, Little? She took Anna back to California with her until Anna insisted on going home, and Sira let her. She didn't want to force her daughter to stay, and Anna was safe with Enrico.

"The reasons for Sira staying in California are her own, but the fact is that years and thousands of miles from her Italy, layer by layer, she applied and then adjusted a mask; not worn to deceive herself, or anyone else, but to place a minute expanse between herself and the world she had to fit into but that she did not always believe in. I'm her best friend,

Little, I watched it all happen from the vantage point of the people who love you but can't make your decisions for you.

"That thin layer was what allowed her to safeguard her Italian heart and mind, and the family that she nurtured and continues to protect every day. She used to say to me that she imagined her country not just as a physical entity but as a marker in her genetic makeup, a key constituent in the blood that ran when she cut herself by mistake, snagged her arm against a branch, or used a knife in the kitchen. A long time passed before she became aware that her heart had betrayed her, minute by year, by absorbing new colors while others seeped out. She was continuously in expansion, sometimes strengthening, occasionally stripping down, as she became something new from all the disparate parts that she was made up of. Sira became a patchwork quilt, and I suppose she saw this as a weakening. Truth is, the heart of Sira today is still the same as the heart of Sira yesterday, a swirl of clean hues.

"She went back to California, and she knew that by doing so, she had opened a new pathway, a separate vein in her family. When we first became friends, she said to me more than once that she hoped she had done no wrong. That used to worry me sometimes, her talk of keeping promises. She could live with hurting herself, Little, but she could not bear the thought of hurting those she loved the most: Enrico, Anna, and then you, once you came along. She desperately wanted to write her own story, live her own freedom, but she never wanted to write the stories of others. This is why I always thought it was funny that people always wanted to entrust her with their stories, lay pieces of themselves on her, as though she could take better care of them. People have always been drawn to her, even though it always looked to me like she herself was drawn to few people. But the ones she loved, she loved—*loves*—more deeply and fiercely than most humans have to give in a lifetime. Her love, for her, has always been a shield, her anger fault lines.

"As soon as I met her I wanted to be her friend, you know. She gave off the air of the untamable, always, but she was so good, and did no harm. She saw things because her eyes were open, knew people because she observed, and listened, and only spoke true words, or none at all. Sira… Sira lingers in your heart, in your mind, no matter who you are or how long she chooses to spend with you. She's always been brave, and didn't look for anybody to tell her what she was. She got divorced in a time when you didn't just *get divorced*; have you thought of the sheer gall that took? And her husband…

"Well, I suppose that is her story to tell. She never even told me much of it, just that they didn't fit anymore, that maybe they never had and she hadn't noticed. After the divorce, she walked like a broken queen, holding her hurts close to her like a sparrow with a twisted wing. I once asked her why she had never remarried—she certainly had no lack of admirers. She smiled at me and said, 'Because I never want to wash another man's socks.' It didn't occur to me until years later that maybe this was not the truth, even metaphorically.

"Sometimes I think I lived my life with so much verve because I wouldn't have dared do otherwise—not with such a thunderstorm as a best friend. A couple of years after I met her, I was in the hospital because my boyfriend at the time hit me so hard I careened down the stairs. I've made stupid mistakes too, Little. Sira showed up and I was so ashamed, I thought she would tell me how dumb I was, and I couldn't bear it; I felt so broken and weak, pathetic. She took one look at me, took off her shoes and crawled into the hospital bed with me, stockings and all, and held me until I had cried it out. She had this little ring back then, simple silver with a turquoise stone embedded into it, and she wore it all the time; said she loved the color. She took it off her finger that day, and handed it to me. Then she said something that I'll always remember. She said, 'When he comes back, you'll have left, following your feet firmly forward, which is only what we are all trying to do; all that will remain for him will be the sensation that you have come and gone. You'll be back on the moon, dancing in the craters, grateful for the chimes of music ringing in the cold air.'

"I thought she had gotten it out of a book. How did she know I needed to hear a melody just then? That was how she told me how she viewed me, as stronger than the situation I was in. She gave me back my identity when it had been taken away. With just those little words, she reminded me, hey, hey, this is you! I know you. That is what a friend does. Believes in you, with no reservations, when you do not believe in yourself, not even a little, tiny bit. It gave me more strength than I could ever have hoped for.

"So those are the pieces of Sira that I can offer you, Little. You'll have to forgive me if this is all that I can give you, but I think it's important so that you can begin to write your own script, weigh out your choices thoughtfully, like marbles in your hand, looking ahead and not behind."

***

The next morning, just after dawn, they drove out toward the coast, Little trying hard to be stoic about having to wake up so early. Betty and Alessandro sat in the front seat, and Little yawned so widely her jaw cracked.

"Why so early?" she had asked, concerned after she said it that it would sound ungrateful. Alessandro had grinned at her widely.

"A bit more suggestive, dawn light, eh?"

Little considered the gossamer light that had surrounded Palazzo Donn'Anna and had to agree.

"Really, though, we want to take Parnassius out, and he doesn't take too well to the heat from the full sun, not so close to summer." But still they would not tell her who, or what, was a Parnassius.

Their country house turned out to be a delightful cottage in the middle of a forest near the sea, with a paddock spread out behind it like a hoop skirt, and a tiny stable attached. She was enchanted.

"Come meet Nassy!" cried Betty, leaping ahead. Parnassius was, as it turned out, a horse. Specifically a German warmblood, seventeen hands, as Betty told her while stroking the soft chestnut nose. "He turns golden in the summer," she whispered reverently, and Parnassius regarded Little with wide, liquid eyes. He had an off-white irregular star on his forehead and a little white snip on his nose, with a big, kind, horsey face.

"He has hooves like dinner plates," noted Little dryly, but Betty gave her a carrot to gift him, and she and Parnassius became friends.

While Alessandro came out with his coffee, which he insisted was far superior to Roman coffee, Betty fussed with Parnassius, who was frisky and excited to be let out. Handing Little a hot cup, Alessandro looked out fondly at his wife.

"I got him for her because she gets melancholy sometimes. I guess I never considered she might miss where she comes from; she never says anything."

"Why the horse?"

"Sometimes you need sweat, clean labor, the companionship of an animal to purify you. And because together, they fly." He turned toward her slowly, raising his hand to clink his coffee cup to hers. "I'm a simple man, myself. Man of the earth, you might say. I don't speak all of your languages, I don't scribble in notebooks or paint, I don't miss any other place because I've never really been many other places. When I'm home, I'm home. So I may not understand the loneliness that haunts her at times, but I know my wife is a butterfly, and I would not dream of cutting her wings." A ghost of a smile played on his chapped lips, and then he turned to go inside, tucking the book in his hands into his back pocket as he went.

Something caught Little's eye. "Wait, Alessandro," she said, reaching out, "what's that on the cover?"

Alessandro pulled out the hand-sized book and handed it to her. "It's about the history of World War II in Italy," he said.

Little ran her finger over the cover, outlining the symbol embossed on the front page, remembering the image flashing by on her television a few months before in San Francisco. She stood stock still, eyes wide open and glazed. Slowly, almost like a convulsion, she pushed past that memory, and found herself in a much earlier moment, years before. She was much younger, opening a drawer and finding a letter. The outside of the letter was imprinted with a symbol that she couldn't place, though now she knew: a perched eagle holding bound sticks with an axe among them. She had pulled it out of her father's drawer and held it up to him. She had not recognized the look on his face.

"What is this, papà?" she had said, reaching for it as he swiftly took the envelope from her hands.

"Darling, yes, the eagle?"

"The sticks. I think I've seen them before."

"I'm sure you have, in a movie or some such. It's a sign of the Ancient Romans, you know, though if I remember correctly, they swiped it from the Etruscans. It symbolized power over life and death. You'll see it scattered a bit everywhere." And he had picked her up and swung her around until her laughter had chased away all thoughts of the bundle of sticks. She had never thought about it again, really, even though she had seen that symbol since.

It was the *fasces*. The symbol of the Fascists.

"Little! Come ride!" Betty called out, and Little turned toward the open forest.

***

Hours later, she sat on the fence, enjoying the solitude and the late afternoon sun, watching the horse sniffle around her. She needed space, when she was thinking, when she was talking. In her mind, she stood in front of the lost Palazzo Donn'Anna, facing its glittering waters. She squinted against the light, determining which of the vessels in the water might be the most secure—something, she remembered, that might carry all manner of things safely through deep waters.

"I miss San Francisco, you know, Nassy," she said to the horse. The horse looked very disapproving at the liberty she had taken with his name. "I feel like I should stay, and I feel like I could go."

"Wouldn't it be marvelous if science discovered a way to inoculate against homesickness?"

Little, startled, turned. Betty was standing at the railing of the paddock. Parnassius, with a happy whinny, trotted over to her immediately, pushing at her hand with the star on his forehead. She smoothed her fingers through his choppy, little bangs.

"I don't know, Aunty Betty. I wonder if that might not change everything." She smiled a little, thought for another moment, and then opened her mouth again. "The other day you said something, about Sira and promises."

Betty nodded. "Yes, I did."

144

"I've had the feeling for some time now that I'm missing something."

To her surprise, Betty nodded again. "Yes."

"Yes?"

"Sira mentioned that you'd been asking some odd questions about your mother."

"Is that all she said?"

Betty grinned at Parnassius. "I don't know if you've noticed, but Sira can be a tad evasive when she wants to be."

Little rolled her eyes. "You don't say. There's just something that I'm not being told. I found this note, back in San Francisco, and zia has been acting oddly, and today I remembered something."

Betty looked interested. "What did you remember?"

"It's just a weird something that might be nothing. As far as you know, did my dad have any connection to the Fascist Party?"

Betty stared at her. "What?" She looked genuinely startled. "No, of course not. Okay, I'm saying that purely out of my knowledge of your father and your family's beliefs, but no, I can't imagine that he did. Of course, there was a time in Italy when it was dangerous to say you didn't agree with the Fascists, but... I would very much doubt that your father had any real affiliation with any of that sort of thing. Not to mention they were kids during the war. Do I think there's some big family secret? Probably, but that's just based on my observations. Do I think it's horrible? No. I can't believe that."

"Maybe you say that because you love them."

"Sure. But I also know them."

"I don't know whether to stay or go, and that makes me feel so guilty that when my sneakers squeak, even *they* sound accusatory. Maybe I don't care what happened. Maybe I just want to go."

"You haven't pushed Sira very hard on this," Betty said to Little, tucking a piece of wayward hair back behind the girl's ear. "I know a time when you might have tried to force the truth out of wherever you could get it."

Little flinched. "I know. Something... something doesn't feel right; like if I force what needs to come out, the truth will be changed in the coming out of it." She shrugged. "And zia feels so much more vulnerable

145

now than she used to when I was younger. I've always thought of her as a giantess. I still think of her that way. But somehow," Little thought back to being in the restaurant in Trastevere and seeing her aunt sitting alone at the table as she walked away, "she feels breakable now. Maybe because she's gotten older. That terrifies me," she admitted, dropping her head. Betty smiled. "Did zia tell you about the note I found?"

Betty nodded.

"It looks like a note that my dad wrote to Delila. I think, anyway. I can't know for sure."

"I notice you don't call her your mother."

"No. Why would I?" Little frowned. Betty nodded. "He seems to be asking forgiveness. He seems to be asking for her to come back. He talks about deceit, and about Delila's father." She looked at Betty questioningly. "Zia says she doesn't know anything about it, other than the fact that Delila eventually left. But how is that possible?"

"Listen, Little," said Betty. "I can't tell you everything you want to know. And that is simply because I don't know most of it. But what I do know doesn't create a whole picture, and I've always left it alone, because frankly, it was none of my business." She put a hand on Little's cheek and did not change expression when the girl moved her face away. "But I do know where Delila is, if you're curious."

Little looked at Betty, completely baffled. "You know where my mother is?"

"Only because she lives in the area. Apparently, she moved back to her father's family in Naples after the separation. To be honest, I don't even really know her. I'm friends with one of her cousins, who also owns a horse, and some years ago I realized who she was. That's all."

Little was silent.

"Would you be able to put me in touch with her?" she finally said, quietly. Betty nodded.

"I asked for the house phone number right before you got here." She replied. "My friend couldn't give me a cell phone number, though I'm not sure why." Little nodded, looking out at the tranquil pasture before her. Betty patiently continued to pet Parnassius.

146

"What do you know about her? Does she live alone?"

"She's separated from her husband," Betty said. "Not your father, someone else. And I know she has children. I don't know anything else."

"She has *children*?"

"Apparently so. What did you think would have happened?"

"I don't know," Little shook her head. "I really hadn't thought of it. Maybe I should continue not to," she ventured. "I don't need to open that door. Delila didn't."

"Well, we try not to make the same mistakes as our parents," Betty joked lightly. Little smiled reluctantly. Her heart ached oddly in her chest at the thought that her mother had other children.

"I have siblings."

"It would appear that way."

"Maybe she has answers for me." She finally looked over at Betty.

"Maybe." Betty looked a little uncertain. Little jumped off the fence, brushing her hands against her jeans to clean them.

"I'll think about it, Aunty Betty. Thanks."

"Sure, Little. You just let me know if you want that number, or if you want me to call for you, or if you need anything from me at all."

She watched, silent, as the young girl walked away, Parnassius following her curiously, his head reaching out to gently nip the back of Little's shirt, as though asking her to turn around.

Chapter 18
Naples, Italy. Present day.

The phone had rung and rung, and with each trill in her ear Little had almost hung up. Betty had volunteered to stand by her side, but she had asked to be alone. In the end, a girl had picked up, her voice young enough for Little to begin making frantic mental calculations of how old she sounded, and if she might be another daughter. And Little had opened her mouth, and no words had come out. The girl had asked repeatedly, *Pronto?*—her voice growing more and more annoyed, until finally, with a huff, she hung up. Little had waited fifteen minutes, seriously considered giving the whole thing up, and then had called back. *Posso parlare con Delila, per favore? May I please speak to Delila?* She had almost asked to speak to her mother, but it felt wrong, especially considering she had not considered Delila much of anything until very recently.

Now Little sat at a café close to Betty's house, studying her hands as she waited for the waiter to bring her a *caffè macchiato*. She wondered if she and Delila might have the same fingers, what she shared in common with this woman who had birthed her. Surely there was something. They could not be strangers. She wondered if something poetic would happen when Delila walked in, if she would recognize her immediately. Did something in your heart recognize your children? What would she feel? Delila, after an initial shocked silence, had agreed to meet Little for coffee. I have so many questions, Little had said, filling the void between the two phones. She had wanted Delila to say something, to express an emotion. I found a letter, Little had said, and received no response from the other end of the line. She had been too afraid to say more, worried that this tenuous hold would shatter. Could you meet me? I'm in Naples. Delila hadn't asked why, or for how long her daughter would be in her city. Delila hadn't said much at all. But she had agreed to meet Little, although when Little had excitedly suggested that afternoon, her response, *non posso oggi—I can't today*—had sounded panicked. When Little had pressed the button to end the call, her fingers had stayed on the screen, and she wondered if she should call Sira. But she suddenly felt full of something that felt like euphoria, pushing on the lining of her stomach, filling her up until she thought she might fly away with the sheer nervousness of it all. She hadn't said anything at dinner, hadn't relayed the phone call to Betty until she needed to ask her where the café was. Should I drive you, Betty had asked, because I can, but Little had said she preferred to walk if it was not too far. She was too buoyed up to sit in a car. Maybe her mother would know everything about what Little needed to know about. She realized only now how much she wanted to know *everything*, have an idea about her father's life from before she herself was an entity in it. Wanted to know what happened to her parents and their relationship.

A shadow fell over the table, and feeling as though a current was running through her, Little looked up.

Chapter 19
Rome. 1996.

It had been a hard year, Enrico reflected as he put the key in the door
to the apartment that faced the Mura Aureliane. Despite their hardships,
he thought that he and Delila were making progress. On nights when he
felt particularly frustrated, he reminded himself that it had, after all, been
his fault, that he must be patient, patient, and build up their trust again.
He still felt that she pulled away in his arms, but could he blame her?
Surely, if he waited it out, she would see how much he truly loved her
and wanted it to work, and then he could tell Sira to bring their daughter
back to them. Sira couldn't possibly be as hard to convince as she acted
over the phone, or be as severe as she had behaved when he had gone
to San Francisco to see Little. That was over six months ago now, he
thought, shifting the grocery bag to his right hand to better jiggle the
key in the lock. Why was it locked, anyway? Delila was home at this time
of day. If he thought about it, she hadn't gone to work in the store that
had been her father's for a long time, letting the employees run it. She
seemed to stay at home most of the time, or, if she was out, she tended
not to tell him where she had gone. He felt it was a punishment, and
took it quietly as such. Maybe he would ask her. Maybe it was time to
discuss uniting their little family again, moving forward past all of this
misunderstanding. He thought with a grimace about the fight they had
had the week before, when he had made the mistake of using that word
in front of her. There was no misunderstanding, she had hissed. There
was the end of a lie.

The door finally swung open and Enrico walked in, balancing the groceries in his arms as he walked the length of the hallway to the kitchen.

"Delila?" he called as he deposited the bags on the kitchen table. "I got the ingredients for *amatriciana*. I thought we could make pasta. Delila?" he called again, popping his head in every room on the way to the living room. Sometimes he found her there, lying on the couch, a book on her chest as she stared up at the ceiling. *"Amore?"*

There was an envelope on the table in the living room. Enrico walked toward it without looking right at it, hoping it might not be there at all. He wondered idly about the significance of envelopes in his life, thought that he might do better if everyone just stopped writing letters.

The envelope looked small in his large, tanned hand. He felt a vacuum of pain opening in his chest. The evening light flickered in from the open window. Enrico glanced up at the little painting on the wall, the one of the garden. He wished he could go there, be unfindable. He found that it was growing harder and harder to breathe. *If I don't open it*, the thought ran through his mind like a mouse, *does that mean she hasn't left me?*

Chapter 20
Naples. Present day.

The girl who stood in front of her was not Delila. Little was sure, because she looked much too young, younger than Little. She had dark hair and eyes, and a stern, straight line of a mouth. She put her hand out for Little to shake. *She must be younger than me*, Little thought as she stood up. A teenager. She shook the girl's hand and sat back down, noting that the girl wore a dark red wrap dress that looked lovely on her.

"I like your dress," she ventured. "Are you going to sit down?"

The girl shook her head, still not smiling. "I can't really stay. I'm Delila's daughter." She eyed Little up and down, and oddly, Little felt judged and found wanting.

"I am, too," she replied, though this was clearly already known.

"Mamma can't make it," she said. *Mamma*, echoed Little soundlessly. The girl looked annoyed. "She explained the situation to me, and she just wants you to know that she appreciates your reaching out, but she just can't open this door." *She appreciates my reaching out*, thought Little. Was this a corporate email?

"You didn't know before?" Little ventured.

"About?"

"Me. About me. About Delila's... your mother's... life before."

"A bit," she admitted, waving a hand as though to dismiss the entire ordeal. "I knew she'd been married and all that before, sure. Anyway, the point is, we're happy, okay? We don't need this."

Little looked at the girl in the dress who had, in one sentence, summarily dismissed her father's marriage and Little's existence. *You're my sister,* she thought, and wondered if it were possible that a part of her DNA reflected itself in the other girl, sparkled in recognition. Then she saw the smile on the neat features of the face she was somehow related to, a smile that seemed more like the grimace of a small animal in a trap. Maybe not. Little stood up.

"You don't need this? *You* don't need this? *I'm her daughter.*"

"Yes," said the girl, who Little realized had not even given her name, "you mentioned that. So am I. We're already a family."

"What's your name?"

"What?"

"Your name. What's your name? Don't you want to know my name? I'm your sister."

The girl shook her head. "My name is Antonietta. To be honest, I don't even know you. You called my mother up out of the blue and demanded to meet her. And frankly I don't care what you want. Just leave it alone, okay? You're upsetting my mother." She used the words "my mother" as though they were a neatly pointed weapon. This was so unfair that Little had no retort, and so said nothing as Antonietta tapped one finger on the table in goodbye, turned around, and walked out.

Chapter 21
Naples. Present day.

"I was so shocked I just let her walk out, Aunty Betty. That was it. That was literally the entire conversation."

Betty and Little sat side by side on the same fence as the week before, overlooking the field in which Parnassius was currently chasing something only he could see, whinnying and bucking in what looked to be pure glee. Little's head rested on Betty's shoulder as she cried. Betty had her arms wrapped protectively around Little's shoulders. They had been discussing the events of the café for the last several days, as Little repeated them over and over, mostly to herself. She had called Delila's number only once, using her cell phone so that the number would be recognizable, so that Delila would be able to know it was her and pick up if she wanted to. She wondered if it had all been a misunderstanding. Delila had not answered, and Little had not called again.

"I thought she had my answers," Little whispered, and Betty gently pushed the girl's hair out of her eyes.

"Sweetheart, with your dad gone, I'm afraid there's only one person who has your answers."

"Zia doesn't want to tell me anything."

"*Non è vero.* It's not true. Promises are like lead, heavy and binding," Betty intoned, "and promises are like smoke, troublesome and insubstantial."

"Where did you hear that?"

"Sira said it to me once. I'm not sure what's going on, Little, but I think your zia is grappling with some promises she made a long time ago. I don't have the answers for you, Little, but I think your aunty might. And I think, if I may give you some advice: You have every right to be hurt by what happened with Delila. I'm hurt *for* you, so I can only imagine what you feel. But you should *never*, not for a second, feel unloved. And you should never feel motherless." She gave Little's shoulder a squeeze, and Little, her head buried in Betty's sweater, smiled for the first time in a week, because it was true.

"I thought it would turn out to be a fairy tale," she whispered into Betty's shoulder.

"It's a fairy tale if you want it to be one. I saw that you've been writing again," Betty said suddenly. "The day you got here, I saw your notebook. Don't worry, I didn't read it—but I'm glad, I'm glad of it."

"It's nothing," said Little, turning toward the dog ambling up to her, a Lab shepherd mix named Mika who lived happily at the stables and nipped at Parnassius's heels whenever the opportunity presented itself.

"It's the opposite of nothing," said Betty, watching the dog sigh contentedly as Little obligingly scratched behind her ears. Betty was absentmindedly twisting the ring she always wore on her middle finger, a simple band, which Little only noticed now had a small turquoise stone set into the middle.

"Aunty Betty? Is that the ring my aunty gave you?" she asked, and Betty looked down and smiled.

"It is."

"Do you think," Little said, reaching out shyly to touch Betty's hand, "that a stone holds power?"

"I think that someone loving you enough to want to protect you in every way they can holds power."

Chapter 22
Orvieto, Italy. Present day.

She couldn't move. In retrospect, she considered, eyeing her empty plate, she probably had not needed to inhale the entire homemade bread basket on top of the black truffle pasta, followed discreetly by the *tagliata*, all dusted with cheese and prosciutto and sprinkled liberally with white wine. Then again, with Orvieto's food and wine famous the world over, it would have been downright reprehensible not to savor every dish the wizened restaurant owner had scurried over to her, puttering with the honey he insisted she try with the cheese. When she had made a joke to him about Orvieto being the inspiration for the Slow Food movement, he had laughed, but only just. "This is how we have always eaten, *signorina*, with respect for that which nourishes us, and love." He'd smiled at her then, pushing the little pot of honey closer to her plate before turning to the next table, red apron securely in place, a badge of his trade.

Little had never known much of Orvieto, tucked on the edge of the Umbria region, but her aunt spoke of it reverently. When she and Sira had been poring over the old map that now stuck out of the back pocket of Little's jeans, the older woman's face had softened at the sight of the name, and so Little had circled it. Getting off at the train station, she had flown over the trees in the funicular necessary to get into the city, surrounded by a family of jocular Austrian tourists. In those moments, in between two places, she had felt as though she could see to the ends of the earth.

A quick Google search had told her that the city had once been a major center of Etruscan civilization, and that one of the popes who took refuge in the city during the sack of Rome had commissioned the deep well of St. Patrick. Little had wandered down to the well that was just at the entrance to the historical city, and was oddly surprised to find it much more of a presence than a well might be expected to be. Deep and dark, it exuded an almost irresistible pull downward. She minded her steps on the long walk down, flashes of shadows intermingled with the openings in the walls that allowed her to see the center. From the bottom, looking up, she could not see where the well ended and the air began again, and she had understood its naming. The well was named for the legend that a site on Station Island in Ireland, named St. Patrick's Purgatory, led down to purgatory itself. She wondered about the sort of city that was guarded by a deep well that seemed an entrance to another place.

Feeling that food was very much in order, she had remembered Sira's advice about finding places to eat; so, instead of hovering near the main piazza to find a worthy restaurant, she deliberately found a quiet street and asked two old men chatting where she might eat *qualcosa di buonissimo*. And so it was that she found herself in this tiny restaurant tucked against the edge of a hidden piazza, promptly humbled by one of the best, and lengthiest, meals of her life. She looked around again as she considered whether there might be room after all for dessert (she was certain that there was).

The owner was a small, sprightly man with a gray beard that exploded around his face like a friendly mane. His wife was, if possible, even smaller, with neatly combed silver hair in defiance of her husband's unruliness. He bounced about to her bidding, and she, seeing Little gazing out into a tiny back garden, left the throne of her kitchen to chat with the tall girl sitting alone. Little was only too happy to share the crisp white wine and listen as the older woman, who introduced herself as Flaminia, explained that their vegetables were all grown fresh in their garden, that her husband had taken over this little place from his father. Looking at the short, plump woman chattering away as though they had known each other for many years, Little thought that there are people who are easily symbolic. This woman was the personification of this wonderful, cozy, little restaurant in this city that seemed more of a town, where the rustic bordered and lived with the mystic and ethereal. She wondered if Sira could have been this sort of woman, running a tiny establishment in a tiny center alongside an uncomplicated, round husband. Though this did not seem like a bad life, she simply could not picture it.

"You'll want the tiramisu, *cara*," Flaminia was saying, "you don't want to wait for next time, and then I'll tell you where to get the best coffee in all of Orvieto. Sadly, it's not here, and that's because Dani won't buy the coffeemaker I specifically told him we needed..." she continued happily on this note for some time until finally instructing Little carefully to walk two streets over and then turn left at the *asinello*. Little looked confused at this, but Flaminia confirmed that yes, indeed she had meant to say little donkey, he didn't move much, and anyway, keep walking straight down from there, you can't miss it.

Little thanked both the owners profusely, shaking their hands and rubbing her tummy in appreciation (and then being immediately embarrassed by this gesture), before slipping out the front door and becoming instantly lost. It didn't matter, as it was a beautiful day in a beautiful place from two hundred years ago, and she was grateful for the sunshine and the sharp breeze, the sound of her feet slapping against the cobblestones. She discovered a large garden that granted her a stunning view of the Umbrian hills that guarded the city. For a while she perched on a low wall, legs swinging, with no one to rush her as she wondered idly if her food would ever digest. The sun was high in the sky and she looked up at it through half-slitted eyes, feeling her muscles unclench. She missed Betty and Alessandro, whom she had tearfully said goodbye to that morning.

As she idly kicked her legs, her mind drifted to the conversation she'd had on the way here. Anna had called and, in her usual grudging voice, told her that since she'd be in the area, Sira had suggested the girls meet in Orvieto and then drive back to Rome together.

"Oh, I don't know Anna, thanks, but I'm actually fine. I don't mind taking the train back, not to mention Orvieto isn't even on the way back from Naples." Little had said, cringing at the thought of an afternoon spent having to make awkward conversation.

159

"You can call Mom and tell her that yourself, then. It didn't sound as though we had a choice," Anna had sniffed, and told her where they could meet later that afternoon. Little had acquiesced, feeling as resentful as Anna, not bothering to ask why she would want to meet in a park.

Ah well, she thought, hopping off her seat. *I'll go meet her in a bit.* Knowing she was putting off seeing her cousin, she went in search of the cathedral, which she'd heard was worthy of the grandest cities in the world (little Orvieto deserved a place on that list). She kept herself lost, and with no set plans and no carefully delineated course of action, she walked the winding, cobbled streets at a lazy pace, taking in the sun-swept corners and shuttered doors, the ancient part of the city where another generation made its home. The farther into the old city she ventured, the more genuine the little stores became, and she found herself perusing a small shop filled with handmade toys, fashioned from wood and painted in bright colors. She bought one, on a whim, wondering whom she would gift it to, and then walked out, turned a corner off of Via dei Magoni, and stumbled onto the mightiest cathedral she had seen outside of a big city.

She was staring at the unusual pastel-shaded lines running up and down the height of the structure with her mouth open when a voice behind her said, "Isn't she beautiful?"

Little turned to find a lean, red-haired girl wearing a tour guide's badge, holding a map and grinning at her. Little smiled.

"She is, but I don't need a tour, thank you."

"Ah, that's alright, I'm on my break anyway. Just couldn't help seeing your expression. First time?"

Little laughed and nodded, happy for the company. "Little."

"Marianne."

"It doesn't look like any other cathedral I've ever seen. The colors are so fantastic. Not as in amazing, although also that—just out of any concept of what I'd think anybody would use for something like this. It's entrancing, and… it just seems so, out of place, in this tiny city." Little took in the array of light within the spectacular nave.

"I always think Italy is one of the only countries that can get away with this sort of stuff. Orvieto had a stretch of time under papal control," Marianne said as she gestured vaguely, with tapered fingers, at the cathedral in front of her. "But what's really cool is that the city has a labyrinth of tunnels in the volcanic rock underneath the ground." She beamed at Little, light eyes flashing, and Little imagined this would be her favorite part to tell tourists. "They stretch tentative fingers, passageways that had been long kept a secret. This city under the city would have led to a safety point outside the bordering walls, for a high-level official of the church to find himself well away from any intruders. Secrets are what we are good at here," she finished with a flourish. Then her smile became impish.

"What do you think of the last line? Overkill?"

"No, I think it's quite good, actually," said Little, rubbing the goose bumps from her arms.

"Oh good, I hoped so. I'm English myself; moved here after I spent a semester abroad and felt so homesick for this place when I went home that I came back first chance I got. I guess these places aren't built to be forgotten," she added, nodding and suddenly looking thoughtful.

Little determined Marianne was weighing whether or not to add that last line to her guide repertoire. Standing in the middle of a piazza she had never before seen nor thought she would ever see, Little smiled to herself because she was talking with a stranger in front of a remarkable structure that simultaneously looked as though it had landed there by mistake and had sprung from the ground, unbidden, entirely at home. For once, instead of feeling out of place or not nearly good enough, she felt as though she had just stumbled into something that had been true of her a long time before, as though there had been a pearl in her pocket all these years and she had only just now rediscovered it, surprised to find its smooth sheen familiar.

"Off to give a tour. It was nice to meet you, Little," she said as they kissed on each cheek. "Thank you for reminding me what it's like to see this for the first time." And with one last grin, auburn hair whipping in the breeze that was picking up, the girl turned and headed toward a group of people who were holding cameras and looking lost.

Little, buoyed by the cathedral and the fizz-filled Marianne, plugged the GPS coordinates Anna had given her into her cell and walked herself over to their meeting spot. Slipping past the open gate into the semi-deserted public garden, she glanced around in appreciation at the thickly green trees, the flowers pushing their way determinedly into the world. The afternoon sun ricocheted off the metal shards that decorated the large clock hanging from one of the rock walls surrounding the area, throwing reflections on the ground. Little watched their jittery dance for a few minutes and then, patting her back pocket to ensure her notebook hadn't fallen out, she turned and found Anna sitting on a bench. She clutched a book in her hands, poised over the pages as though whatever its words contained would cause her to take flight any moment.

"So what brings you to Orvieto?" Little said, slowly walking forward, not wanting to interrupt the other girl's reading trance.

"Nothing," said Anna, snapping her book shut as she looked up at Little. "I just wanted a quiet place to read. To forget myself."

Little's nose twitched in surprise. It was something she might do herself. She nodded, holding her hand out to help Anna get up. Anna looked at it for a moment before taking it and hauling herself to her feet.

"Ooof, I've been sitting for a while. I'm all critchety."

"Critchety?"

"Full of critchets," Anna explained, throwing her head back and laughing. Little frowned, not with anger but because she felt unbalanced; her cousin was perpetually serious, angry. Maybe the sun had warmed her up. Remembering the coffee bar recommendation from Flaminia, Little suggested an espresso and began meandering back to where she thought the restaurant she had eaten was.

"We're looking," she said, "for a little donkey."

Anna nodded. "Of course we are."

They walked for a bit in silence, until Anna said, "You know Sira went to the house in Sperlonga for a bit?" Little nodded. "I'm going to go and stay with her for few days. I'll drop you off in Rome and head south."

"Cool," Little replied. Anna looked at her.

"You know, Little, I get that you have a lot going on, but you don't always have to have such a *muso lungo*."

"*I* have a long face? You practically have a copyright on the facial expression."

Anna snorted. "Shockingly, you're not the only one in the world with preoccupations."

"Actually Anna, I'm more than aware of that—you're the one who seems to struggle with the concept that someone other than you exists," Little bristled. To her surprise, Anna shrugged.

"Let's not fight again, Little. It's a beautiful day," she said, gesturing around herself, "and I don't want to ruin it."

"Okay," Little replied, feeling guilty and not knowing quite why. She looked more closely at Anna, whose face seemed relaxed, almost… content.

"Anna? Did something happen to you?"

Anna smiled, for what Little considered might be the first time in several years. "Not really. I just really enjoy being out in the countryside. I love living in this country, and being in places like Orvieto reminds me of that." She looked closely at her younger cousin. "You used to as well, you know."

Little shrugged, ready to clam up. "That was a long time ago. I mean, I like it here, and I feel oddly at home, but also, I don't want to be bogged down by this place, with all its predetermined customs and traditions and… roots."

"They're roots. Those are the things you build from," said Anna, not unkindly.

"And papà," Little went on, her stomach knotting at the idea that he was nowhere that she could go, "he's gone. And it's easier not to feel that, when *I'm gone*." She hadn't meant to say that out loud, hadn't actively thought it. "And there are all these memories that I just can't work out." Before she knew it, she was telling Anna about the symbol, the odd connection, and Sira's strange reaction. She stopped short of telling her about the nonmeeting with Delila, because it still made her flush with embarrassment. To her surprise, Anna listened intently. "I just feel very lost, I suppose," Little said, wrinkling her nose at the cliché.

"You don't look that lost," said Anna somewhat dryly. "You look like you always look, like you've taken aim and you're plunging headlong into an adventure that nobody is sure about except for you."

"Maybe I look confident because I picked up a tan," said Little pensively, feeling her face. Anna threw back her head and laughed, the sound pealing off the stone walls around them.

"Are you missing a homing signal?" Anna asked then, more seriously.

Little's eyebrows knitted together. "A homing signal?"

"Yes. You know. That feeling inside when you close your eyes and search for home and know it's there. It's not always a place. Sometimes it's a person." Little looked puzzled, not just at the statement but at its provenance. Anna flapped her hands at her. "Go on then, try it."

Little closed her eyes for one, two, three beats. Then she opened them again.

"Do you feel lonesome?" Anna asked. Little looked at her to see if she was making fun of her, but Anna's face was serious.

Little considered the question. "No. No, I don't. But I feel more than one place, people, calling to me. That's the problem. I suppose I see Italy more than I did before, but California is still there. It's still tangled up in there. San Francisco. Mill Valley. Sausalito. My friends, my school. The smell of the ocean, which smells nothing like the sea here."

"Want to know what I think, for once?" said Anna.

"I do."

"I think having more than one homing signal is a grand problem to have. I think that maybe the only bad homing signal is a lost one."

"Anna?"

"Mmmhmm?

"Have *you* lost a homing signal?"

"No," replied Anna, thoughtfully. "No. But having you here," Anna pulled in a breath, "you know, Little. It was just us. Just us. And then you came along. And it was like you were the kid she'd been waiting for. And it's always like that, in a way. Every time you come around."

Little sat very still. Anna did not look at her cousin, focusing on the view that unfurled before them, a patchwork quilt of hills and trees. Little thought she smelled something musty, as though something were being shaken out that should have been sorted long before.

"Should I apologize for that? I can," she added quickly, "if it helps." She was surprised to find that it was true.

Anna sighed. "No. I just wanted you to know why it might be hard for me sometimes." She pulled something out of the dark brown leather saddlebag she wore swung over one shoulder.

"Here," she said. "I found this tucked in zio's things a while back. I hadn't thought it was important then, but I saw it the other day and, well, I thought you might want to see it." Little knew then that Anna felt sorry that she had kept Little's birth bracelet from her. Before seeing what Anna had in her hand, before she lost her courage to apologize, she spoke.

"Anna," she said, "I'm sorry I broke Dad's Pinocchio. I honestly didn't mean to." The image of the smashed wooden doll on the floor of their house, of Anna's genuine exclamation and crestfallen face, had followed her through her time in Italy, and now she felt better for having accepted the responsibility. The older woman looked at Little, hazel eyes warming, and smiled a little forlornly.

"Here," she said, handing Little a yellowed envelope, "take it. Now that you've told me about the symbol and my mother acting strange, it seems even more relevant."

The envelope was old and crumpled, and looked like it had gotten wet at some point, because the ink that had once formed words had smeared and dried into shapeless, faded puddles on the page. With one finger, Little gently traced the only outline that was left visible: The fasces had been messily scrawled on the top left-hand corner. She looked up at Anna.

"I think this is the same letter I saw when I was a kid. Do you recognize this symbol?"

"Sure, Little. It's the fasces of the *fascisti*." She shrugged. "Did you not know what it was?"

"Well, sure, I mean, I'm sure I did but it didn't connect until I saw Alessandro's book."

"Sometimes I do wonder about your American education. Did you guys even study?" Anna rolled her eyes, and Little rolled them back at her.

"I received a stunning, top-notch education. Now shh." She slowly opened the envelope to find a piece of paper tucked inside, but that was illegible, too.

"Why would Dad even keep this? There's nothing in it." Frustrated, she flipped the page over. Anna shrugged.

"It was in a drawer of the little bedside table by his bed when he died. Whatever it was, it was important enough for him to keep it. But I think there was some significance," she pointed to the symbol still visible on the envelope, "because once, when I was really little, I overheard zio talking to an old man who had come to the apartment in Rome. They were arguing about something. I don't know what because I couldn't hear much even though I had my ear pressed to the door of the room they were fighting in."

"Of course you did."

"Hey. You're lucky little Anna did, because it's the only info you seem to be getting. Anyway, they were arguing, and by arguing, I mean I remember it because the man kept raising his voice and zio kept shushing him, and then at the end the man had thrown the door open and I was standing there. He pushed right past me; didn't even acknowledge the fact that a tiny blonde kid had been glued to the door." Anna glanced at Little, who was still flipping the page back and forth, trying to make out any words in the confection of smeared black on the old paper. "And while he was walking out, your dad tried calling him back, and the man turned around and called him a *fascista.*" Little froze.

"What the *hell?*"

"Yeah." Anna turned to face Little, who had stopped walking. "He spat the word at him. Your dad looked like the man had hit him in the face. He jerked backward, and the guy stormed out." Anna studied Little's face closely. "Little, surely you don't take this stuff seriously. I mean, honestly, your father? I can't imagine anyone *less* likely to be a Fascist."

"Yeah?" said Little, remembering now all of the things she had read, at one point or another, about that war. "Except it isn't always the people you think it's going to be, right? And then why that reaction from Dad?" As she spoke the words, Little stilled, remembering the words in the other letter she had found. *I will not tarnish your memory of your own father in hopes of restoring myself with you.* Was there a connection between Delila's father and what Anna was telling her now?

"I don't know, Little. Maybe it's time to ask my mom. But zio, he wouldn't have done anything bad." Anna's hands closed.

"You knew him better than I did," said Little, realizing how hard it was for her to say so out loud. "Maybe it's easier to find that trust."

"Maybe it is," admitted Anna, resuming the walk. "And I know it's not the same, but I can tell you stories, you know. Isn't that part of the point of memories? Sharing them? And zio and my mother, when they were younger, wow, what a pair they made. There was this one time, with this priest…" Anna burst into laughter. "Let's go find that coffee place, Little."

And, surprisingly, she took Little's hand, and Little, equally surprisingly, did not pull away.

TRAVELS FORWARD

Chapter 23
Rome. Present day.

There is a rumor of a secret garden in the middle of Rome. The real question is, what middle? Like any cohesive place worth its weight in salt, Rome has many middles, at least as many as it has beginnings, and possibly more than it has endings. I know. Don't roll your eyes. It really is there. Is it so hard to believe that the city itself may need a spot of peace among the cacophony it breeds within its borders every day? You can't drive there (you wouldn't find parking anyway), but you can take your chances with walking, if it wants to be found. If you choose to wander somewhat aimlessly, your odds will be even better. They say if you lose focus slightly when you are on the train heading to the airport, and try not to pay too much attention looking out the window, you can catch a glimpse of the gates from far off. Then again, I don't even know who "they" are, or what they say, so don't rely on what I've heard.

Little looked up from writing in her notebook and gazed, unfocused, out the café window. Her center felt as unmoored as this garden. When she had gotten back to the apartment in Rome, she had found it empty. It left her feeling oddly bereft. With Sira escaping the Roman heat at the house in Sperlonga, Little was on her own. She sat in the living room for the better part of an hour, looking around at the pictures on the walls, the ones she had never really looked at properly or wondered about. They must have been hung there by her father. There was one in particular that intrigued her, a small oil painting that held a place right next to the window, and so was almost always in the light. It was a little gated garden, all painted with vivid greens and a splash of blue for the creek running through it, and tall stone pines waving in the background. It looked as though there would always be a breeze, and a place to sit and read.

Eventually she had set out into the mugginess of Rome to lose herself as thoroughly as possible, for once not in search of answers, but rather cloaked in the comforting knowledge that here was something bigger than she was. She had stopped to write down a note about the little garden in the living room, and now she stood up from her seat, paid for her espresso, and headed out with no particular direction in mind.

She found herself in Piazza Mattei, a place she had loved as a little girl and had avoided since then. This, she reflected, taking in her beloved turtle fountain, was where her mother had once hit her. She must have been very small, because her mother had looked so large above her, and it must have been cold, because the push had felt muffled, though the slap had not. The next memory had been of an enraged Enrico scooping her up in his arms, shielding her, his face contorted, pushing into the café across the street where she had had hot chocolate and he had stroked her face. Sira had arrived, and there had been some discussion, at some point, between her and her mother, but by then Little had been more focused on her hot chocolate. And that moment had set what she considered the truth for the rest of her life: Her father and Sira had been her powerful protectors against whatever her mother must have been. Then she and Sira had set off on their grand San Francisco adventure, and that had been that. Her mother had faded into the background of her life, an asterisk in the very beginning, where her memories were fuzziest. She thought of the other letter, the typewritten one, a wayward clue that had found its way to a pile of old documents in her apartment in San Francisco. *What are the odds*, she thought. She turned around and took in the fountain one more time, pushed her hair back from her face and sighed. She couldn't make up the parts she didn't know. Fourteen years later, she knew the only person who could possibly give her the pieces that were missing.

Chapter 24
Rome. Present day.

She was dreaming, and in her dream the night hung heavy and dark, like a pewter cloak glistening on the girl's back as she wandered the empty, dusky streets. She was searching for her name everywhere, in Rome, in Florence, even in the lost Venetian waters; would climb into and out of the canals if she had to, and she would call out silently, because she did not know what she was calling to, or calling for.

She found herself, with no warning, in the arena of the Colosseum, but not like it was today. No, these were wooden planks under her feet, like in times of old, and surrounding her was no half-ruin, but the wall that had been called Podium. The night chilled her, and the only company to keep here were the hundreds of thousands who had had their lives torn from them. She stood in the middle of what had been used for both theater and slaughter, and looked up at the night sky and the stars and searched desperately for answers there, for rest and for certainty. She looked around herself, at the silky ghosts clinging softly to her sleeves, and wondered if they still had their names, and if they knew how the whole world spoke of those who had died here, that nobody mourned them anymore, and maybe never had. With sad eyes, she brushed their memories from her clothing and left that place.

When she came to Burano, one of the islands that belong to Venice, where they make the finest lace, the night had become so inky it was hard for her to see ahead. She looked about at the muted grays of the walls and seemed to remember that the homes of the fishermen, in daylight, were awash with an infinite array of colors. She walked over the rounded wooden footbridges that spanned the miniature city and laid out a warm blanket by the water, and let the lagoon lap at her feet. And she called out soundlessly for her name, but it did not come.

She walked and walked, and though her mind was turning her back, she decided that her steps should always point forward, so forward she went, down a long Tuscan lane rimmed on either side by cypresses, with the lights of the walled town of San Gimignano twinkling at her in recognition in the distance. But what was her name? Had she had one when she was awake? The trees on each side of her, stirred by the wind, sleepily shook themselves out, and the girl went on.

Little, in her bed far away, smiled and turned around in her sleep.

And then she was in a canyon city made of rocks and knew she had found her way to Matera, in the ancient center that was one of the first human settlements in Italy, rolling gently up the slope of a ravine. She shivered slightly because there is no other city like Matera, the yellow carved place of the Sassi, where people go to remember that some human things are not built of metal, cement, or even marble. She felt the deep, raw power that surged and ran underground, and judged herself too small to dare ask of it a thing so inconsequential as her own name. Maybe if she had bigger questions, about time or space or loss, about stone that carves and protects but does not break. But as it was she bowed her head slightly, out of respect. In her mind, that which comes from other ages, like that which comes from book, pencil, or brush, is sacred. She turned to go.

When she looked up she blinked in surprise at the familiar sight, for she was back in Rome and looking squarely up at the Arch of Constantine, which stands next to the Colosseum and is the first thing you see when walking down the road that connects the two to Circus Maximus. Here, slowly, she grew aware that she was not alone, that there were other women with her, walking and not speaking, but they did not feel alien to her, and so she was not afraid. Some of them were walking ahead, glimmering as the moonlight passed through their swirling skirts, and while some seemed very old, there were those who were younger and much more nimble, walking with less regal elegance but with their heads thrown back almost in defiance. Still some were walking behind her, and when she turned her head to look, these too she could not see clearly, and they did not seem to be paying her any attention, though they acknowledged her with small smiles while they looked elsewhere. There was one woman, with wide, dark brown eyes, who walked beside her, and though silent like all the rest, she was also the only one to look directly at the girl, for the girl, though free, carried this city deep within her own self. And the girl knew then that these were her past, present, and future places of belonging, and that she would love and find herself in endless of these in her life, some lived in and some not, some corporeal and a few that she would dream, places she would build in her imagination. As soon as the realization bloomed in her sleepy awareness, the women turned to smile, and with a rustle of silk and cloth that sounded like thunder, they were all gone.

And then, there she was, and she *had* been here before. This was Rocca Calascio, the mountain fortress that she had found once on an excursion while she was in the region of Abruzzo, the lonely stronghold surrounded by lemon-hued moors and whipped by wind; she had later been told that she had stumbled across the highest fortress of the Apennine Mountains. The imposing gray stone skeleton of the Rocca behind her, she walked up one of the wide paved roads until she was lost in the hills behind the towers, and she sat on the highest, loneliest rock and looked out over the upland washed white with moonlight and asked the wind how she might find her name. She felt it surround her in response, buffeting her in reassurance. *I don't know*, the wind sighed all around her, *but I can take you where you can find it for yourself, time you can spend in the discovery of all the names of your life, and this opportunity is the real gift. Be worthy.* So the wind picked the girl up and swept her into the clear night, and instead of resisting or fearing the fall, the nameless girl opened her arms wide and greeted the voyage as her own. When she glanced down she finally found that her wings unfurled after all, and that there was air to propel her still upward, upward and forward, and she thought she could hear the gentle, pealing sound of a laughing breeze. And so she worried about nothing, which was unlike her, and let the wind carry her.

In her home, with a gentle start, Little woke up.

175

Chapter 25
Sperlonga. Present day.

Although tempted to rent her 500 again, Little took the train to the house in Sperlonga. As she walked through the station she realized she was growing quite fond of these meeting places, and had somehow learned to not grossly overpack, a major victory in itself. She wore sandals and a light blue summer dress she had bought in Orvieto. In the pocket was her notebook fashioned of Florentine leather, and around her neck hung a light gold chain, very nearly invisible, with a delicate delineation of the state of California.

She was comfortable like this. She placed one finger underneath the collar of her dress and pressed the outline, just hard enough for it to leave its reflection on her skin. Then she pulled out her notebook and wrote, in hurried letters: *a depiction, like our ornaments so often are, of that which is in our hearts.* Just one line, to herself, so that she would remember it. Then she closed the little book and glanced back up.

"Hey, Little," Anna walked up behind her, placing a hand lightly on the younger woman's shoulder. "You look good."

Little raised her hand to her newly dark hair. She'd dyed it a shade or two richer than her natural hair color the day after she had come back to Rome. She had been instantly won over by the hue's name: Chocolate. She had grown tired of the blonde, and if she had to be honest, it had never really suited her complexion. She'd also spent a good hour soaking off the gel French tips she'd gotten used to having, cut her nails short, and replaced the sober white with a bright purple shade. For a moment, she thought she remembered a dream she'd had about colors, and smiled to herself. Running about Italy these last weeks, without a car to drive everywhere, had given her muscles in her arms and legs that she hadn't had before, no matter how many hours she had spent in the well-groomed, air-conditioned San Francisco gyms, and she realized she rather liked the idea of having her body be a result of a life well lived.

"*Grazie*, Anna," she said, grinning as she hauled her bag into the trunk of Anna's car.

The night before, she had just hung up with Marta, who had called with an interesting proposition, when the phone had rung again. Anna, on her way back to Rome from Sperlonga in the morning, offered to pick Little up at the station and drop her off back at the beach house.

"How is zia?" Little asked while they drove.

"She insisted I must eat seven times a day or I would simply perish."

Little burst out laughing, and then Anna was laughing, too.

"The other day," Anna said, "I walked in on her playing an aria on the stereo in the living room—'Nessun Dorma' from Turandot. You know, the Puccini opera?" She glanced over at Little, who nodded. "Anyway, her eyes were closed." Anna closed her own eyes for a moment. "And she didn't even notice me walk in because she was so absorbed in it. When it was over, and her eyes opened, I sat down and asked her who her favorite composer is. And all she replied was, 'Puccini says the things I cannot say, but Verdi makes me strong.'" She turned to look at Little. "I was completely blown away," she admitted, and Little knew the feeling.

"When we went through zio's things in Rome, do you remember there were some old playbills?" Anna went on.

"Yes, I left them on the shelf, actually," Little replied.

"Do you think they ever went together?"

"You would know better than me," Little admitted.

"I don't know. Maybe they talked about opera together."

"Maybe they did."

"I don't... I don't really love opera," Anna admitted.

Little smiled. "I don't, either. Don't tell Sira I told you this, but sometimes, it's kind of..."

"Boring?"

"Not all of it. Maybe after the first half hour?" Anna started to laugh, and Little followed suit.

"Are you going to talk to Mom about the letter?"

"Yes," Little replied, looking out the window. "About everything." Oddly, it didn't seem to bother her as much as it had before.

Anna nodded.

"You know, this woman I met while I was traveling called me last night," Little began, not sure if she and Anna had yet found their way back to a place where they could give each other advice, "asking me to write a piece for her local paper. She's one of the editors. Said she thinks I have an interesting take on things, on Italy. She said I could write about it any way I wanted." She looked over at Anna, who nodded.

"That sounds right up your alley, Little."

"Yeah?"

"Totally. Are you going to do it?"

Little was thinking. About Barbara, who was desperately qualified but couldn't find a job, yet never lost hope; about Sira, who hadn't wanted to force Little to come back to Italy because she feared there wouldn't be opportunities for her here; about Marta and Rolando, and their olive grove. About the Carli family shop. Her father's story. The man from the metro. About Betty, smiling when she saw Little's handwriting scrawled across a page. About how writing etched itself into her heart and made her feel whole, with something to give, and also light like a balloon, so that she might reach any height she chose.

"Yes," she said. Her fingers itched with ideas. Anna nodded, satisfied.

"Good. We're here," she said, pulling the car up to the gate of their house. They touched cheeks but didn't hug, and when Anna slipped back into her car, Little felt a little tremble underneath her feet, as though chasms were slowly beginning to close. She waited until Anna had headed back down the road, then unlocked the gate and eased it open, thinking of the endless times she had come in the summer to greet her father.

She let herself in the front door and there was Sira, puttering in the kitchen.

Unexpectedly, a lump rose in Little's throat as though she might cry. She dropped her bag and enveloped her aunt in a hug, the bear hugs that always made Sira laugh; she had never been a physical person, but Little insisted on it, and Sira had grown to love the girl's exuberance in physical comfort.

"I made you food!" Sira said, laughing. It was the same as saying, I missed you, and I'm so glad you came home with a smile.

"Thanks, zia, I'm famished," Little answered. *I missed you, too. Thank you for being here when I came back.*

"I love your hair like that." *I'll always be here, in one way or another.*

Sira touched her niece's hair lightly, then turned toward the table. "While Anna was here in the last few days, we talked to a real estate agent. If you give the okay as well, we'll put the house up for sale now." *It doesn't matter how used to starting over you are, it's always hard.*

"Good," said Little, smiling, and Sira looked up at her encouraging tone. *I'll always be here, too.* Sira met her niece's gaze, and her eyes beamed.

"I think you have questions, Little," Sira said, and Little wondered if Betty or Anna had mentioned something. She nodded.

"Did you hear about Delila?" Little asked, and she thought for a fleeting moment that she saw Sira's eyes harden.

"Yes. I'm very sorry she treated you that way." Sira looked as though she had more to comment on her ex-sister-in-law's behavior, but bit her tongue.

"There are some things I don't understand, zia. I'm worried that my father was a Fascist. I'm worried that I didn't know him enough to be able to decide for myself whether that's possible or not. I don't understand what happened with my father and mother. I thought these entanglements, they were confusing, like roots overgrowing one another, tangled and ready to trip me. I thought that if I stayed away, I could grow on my own. But Anna said something to me the other day, about roots. And she's right. We can grow from them. I need roots, too, or how will I hold fast against the wind? But I need to know what I don't know. Please."

Sira, looking at Little's wide brown eyes, heard her brother's words as though he were standing next to them now, instead of years before. *Sira,* he said. *You have been the keeper of everything of importance to me.*

She nodded.

Chapter 26
Sperlonga. Present day.

"Your father was not a Fascist, Little. This is the first thing I need you to know. He was never really about politics, and he was also a child during the war. Remember the stories I told you about the hunger, my mother coming home with a carrot, your father coming home with food and saying he stole that food from the German trucks? I think even more than the hunger it was the fear of the hunger, the looming of it. Everywhere you looked back then, there were tragedies, and it was a slippery slope. People lived in fear of that moment, that turning of precarious luck to doom. When he was about nine years old, Enrico provided information to the Fascist Party in Rome in return for food for our family. He told them that a man who had a shop nearby, a man named Beppe Selinti, had double-crossed the regime by selling them goods from his shop at a higher price and making fun of the Fascist soldiers behind their backs. This was true. It was also true that Beppe Selinti was an incredibly unlikable man, that he had once called my father scum for having Jewish friends. This was just before the war began, when anti-Semitic sentiment was something to be advertised in order to keep your family safe. Beppe had chosen my father because he knew him to be a quiet man, and wrongly assumed that meant he was a pushover. He had stopped my father in the street one day and yelled in front of the whole street that my father was a Jew-lover. My father, I am told, looked him squarely in the face and told him that was indeed true, that he was proud of having friends from all backgrounds. If that scene had taken place six months later, my father would have been killed for saying something like that. Beppe spat on him in the street. This was a story that Enrico remembered, a grudge he held though his own father did not. Still, I do not excuse your father. Beppe Selinti's store was forced to close. He was beaten very badly. I didn't know anything about all this. I don't think anybody ever did. Selinti was shamed and Enrico so full of guilt he never would have dared say anything about what had happened. All I remember is that my brother grew surly, rarely went outside anymore, and that we had very little food. My parents eventually moved us to Narni, as you know. I do not think they ever knew what had happened.

"Years later, when the war was a shadow that we had the opportunity and privilege of forgetting, your father told me he was marrying a woman named Delila Selinti. I knew her as the daughter of Beppe Selinti, the merchant. He had opened another shop after the war, although he never did well. Your father had never so much as mentioned Delila to me before. I knew he did not love her, and I didn't buy his story. And so he told me the truth. That Beppe Selinti had told Enrico that he had been his ruin during the war, that he had never managed to get back on his feet and so had become a failure of a man, and that nobody would marry his daughter because he himself had nothing to offer. Delila, to Beppe's horror, had secretly harbored feelings for your father. And so Beppe had decided that they would get married. Your father eventually wrote Beppe a letter that he would marry Delila, and so make amends. I told Enrico that this was ridiculous, that so many years later he could not possibly be blamed for the man's ruin, that he was being tricked into marrying a woman he did not love; but he refused to listen to me. He had felt guilty for many years. He thought he could make Delila happy.

"Of course, years later, when you were a child, Delila found the letter. It was among her father's things, and she had been going through them after he passed away. She lost her mind, Little, because you see, whatever her awful father had cooked up and my stupid brother had gone along with, Delila had not known about. She had married for love. And I believe Enrico had fallen in love with her too, but had kept Beppe's secret. Out of fear? To not taint her relationship with her father? Or was it cowardice?

I don't know. Though it wasn't meant to be, it was a cruel thing. She confronted your father in Piazza Mattei. You know what happened then. The letter ended up in the fountain, and for God knows what reason I grabbed it out of there. I don't know why your father kept it after that. The only thing left visible was the fasces symbol that Beppe had scrawled on it in an act of mockery when he had come to see your father and gloat after he had received the letter. For a long time, I damned that letter, but now I think Delila had a right to know. I told Enrico that not telling the truth warps people's ability to make conscious choices, but he asked me never to speak of it, never to allow this to mar your image of him. I never did. Since Delila turned... violent... after she found out the truth, Enrico asked me to take care of you for a while, until he could get a handle on the situation. He never managed that. She left, after about a year. He tried to bring her back, asked her to be a mother, but she simply behaved like she no longer cared. Maybe she really didn't. Again, your father asked me to let you live in peace of this knowledge. And then the lie had lain dormant for so long, and I wondered if it could possibly matter, but more than anything, I knew that by guarding my brother's secret, I had become a part of it. And I didn't want you to be ashamed of me either, Little. I told myself that you needed stability and not old family secrets. I told you bits and pieces of the story. And that was my mistake, inadvertently deciding for you what was important and what wasn't. And then you started asking questions about things I thought we had tucked away. Why now? I can only tell you what I think. I think that it was time. And I admit that I am relieved.

"The other day I read the story you found, one of your father's. The one he named 'Starlings.' And then I knew that I had to talk to you, if only so that you could understand your father's story. That's about Delila's family shop, you know. I'm sure of it. She had a nephew, awfully cute little boy. Enrico adored him. Beppe Selinti's second shop eventually shut down. Delila had run it for some time, but even before she left your father she had let it go to ruin. I don't know what happened to the nephew. I didn't ask. I was so busy covering my own family's flanks, I never thought to bother with Delila. I know Enrico secretly harbored a hope that she would come back one day, and that he could put things right between his daughter and her mother. She never did. So your father had to live with never being able to fix his mistake. It kept him up at night.

"I never considered Delila, really. I felt bad for her, sure, but not too bad; not once I knew that she had allowed herself to become physically violent with you. But I never fleshed her out in my own mind. She was a bit player on the stage I set up for my family. Until that day at the fountain when she struck you. Then all your father and I could think of was to protect you. It's a dangerous thing, Little, not to take people into account. Nobody took Delila into account. Not her father. Maybe not even Enrico, although he was awfully kind to her. So that letter you found, that was one of many that your father wrote to her. Some he read to me over the phone, asking me for advice. Some he sent, and some I think he did not. There was another line in that letter you found, or maybe in another one, that I never commented on, but will never forget. He said, 'because it is so hard for a child to grow up motherless.' I resented that, Little, though maybe it was not my right.

"And that, truly, is what there is to it. Do you think you can forgive me, Little?"

Chapter 27
Sperlonga. Present day.

The next morning, Little let herself into the garage, rolling the great doors back and finding herself in what her dad jokingly used to refer to as his office. She hadn't been here in a long time. She had spent the night thinking about the things she now knew. The same written word that she had learned to love through her stories were the way in which her mother's life had been ruined; and Little now knew how words could hurt as well as heal. She thought she could take the lesson and make the best of it. Despite knowing that she could have, indeed, had the right to be angry, somehow she wasn't. What she felt was disappointment that the unveiling of this secret had not helped her discover her father. Despite feeling relieved that she now knew the truth, the truth didn't make her feel closer to him.

She walked to his desk, still littered with wood shavings and the occasional pencil, and when she lifted her eyes to the shelf above, there were more papers, just as Anna had told her there would be. She pulled them out, coughing at the dust, and looked around for a chair. Finding none, she walked to the middle of the room and sat down, the papers spread before her. They were mostly like what she had found in Rome: pieces of his life, work notes and bills that had been paid, brochures from concerts and shows, letters from her when she had been very little, and the occasional soccer game stub from when he had gone to see his favorite team, AS Roma. Again, she found a couple of old playbills, these for *Madame Butterfly* and *La Traviata* (Puccini and Verdi again, a little voice

185

said in the back of her mind), and these she set aside to show Anna later. At the very bottom of the stack, she found it, just the one story—a story of self, and of them all.

Io ho il diritto ed anche la responsabilità
(The Colosseo, the Golden Gate, and everything in between that matters)
(It all matters)

As an Italian, I have the duty to cherish my country and my people, to never belittle what we are capable of, and to always remember our history—both to honor the astounding achievements but also to remember and not flinch from the mistakes, in the hope and determination that we are not to make them again.

I have the right to be grumpy before my first espresso, and especially if my favorite cornetto is sold out at the bar in the morning. If you're all out of my favorite filling, I have the right to throw something at you. I'm kidding, I don't. No, but really, there isn't even a little one left?

I have the right to fresh food and to clean water, and the duty to be outraged when others do not. I also have the duty to not let my outrage be all that I offer this initiative.

I have the duty to support small businesses, and the right to snub conglomerates if I wish to.

I have the duty to respect the elder generations that have come before me, and I have the right to expect that respect in return.

I have the right to say that I don't trust my political system, but then I have the duty to suggest changes, to be part of the solution and not the problem.

I have the right to expect more, and the duty to not assume that others will go and get it for me.

I have the right to honor the spaces around me and the duty to never leave any place or any person in a lesser state than when I arrived.

I have the right to impossible dreams, and to never let anybody make me feel that I cannot set out after them. I have the right to my path, to love who I want, and the *right* to expect that my nation will extend this liberty to everyone else, to let everyone love *who* they want and *how* they want, as long as they are never harming another. And if my neighbors, or my city, my country, or the whole world blocks this right, then I have the *duty* to stand up and say that it is not fair.

Peace! I demand it! I demand the liberty to fuss over my future without concerning myself over whether or not I will have one, to have the freedom of building something for myself and my loved ones with no fear in my heart that a stranger could come and take it, or them, away, for a concept I know nothing of and have certainly not subscribed to.

Freedom. Clear blue sky, a pen, a notebook. The office, missing the train, head back and laughing over aperitivo. The Colosseo, the Golden Gate Bridge, every little thing in between that means something to any one of us, to all of us. Shadows, go away from here. I demand. To know no terror. For all of us, always.

I have the duty to be proud, and to stand tall. I have the duty to stand up when we do something wrong, but also when something wrong is done to us, whether that be from outside or comes from within. I have the duty to do this using my voice and my mind, and never my hands. I have the duty to never besmirch my people or the name of my family by being violent, or intolerant, or unkind.

I have the incredible right to open my mind and make mistakes, to do my best now and also to do better next time.

I have a duty as an Italian. But this is the secret that we hear from the tippy tops of mountains and standing at the bottom of a canyon and waking up in our beds in the morning. This is for all of us, every person and every country, both to the singular spaces and cultures that we feel we belong to and cherish, and also to everyplace, as global citizens. Our borders, after all, are only the ones that we have drawn.

I have the right *and* the duty to let my feet take me where they may, to explore, to see new places, to meet new people, to share my stories and also, always, to listen to yours.

Chapter 28
Sperlonga. Present day.

Some keys are smooth, well-made things, all soft, rubbed edges, whirring when they fit in their lock, turning with a satisfying click. Some are jagged and sharp, rough-hewn as though made by error, with little thought or care. They, too, open the doors they were created for. Little's own particular key clicked into place then, sitting on the ground of the garage, her father's papers fanned out on her lap, and she knew that this was what was left to her of a man whom she had loved, despite never knowing him enough. Through his stories, she was having a conversation with her father that they'd not had in real life. Or maybe she just hadn't been listening to him then, she wasn't sure.

Not nothing; everything. Not nowhere; everywhere. She was filled with a feeling that she did not at first recognize, but then realized was pride: pride at her father's words, that she was the daughter of this man, that she was the niece of Sira—no, no—that she had been *raised by* Sira with all of the love that implied, that she was a girl who wrote like her grandfather. She got up, turning to face the door, and began, slowly, to walk out. Then she came back, smoothed out the rest of the papers and put them back where she had found them. Those were parts of him, too, pieces of his every day. His story, and the booklets for Anna, she tucked under her arm. She glanced at the outline of the boat that stood against the far wall, the last relic of one of his favorite pastimes, to build things. Her heart gave a sudden, painful lurch, and tears burned in her eyes but did not fall. She smiled a little, then.

"Hey, papà," she felt silly as she spoke, but she took a breath. "Did you leave that story here for me? I hear you, Dad. I wish…" Here she grimaced a little. "Well. I went on a trip. I think you would have liked that I went. I wish we could talk about it. Talk about it really, not like this." She gesticulated, taking in the cavernous room where her words were reverberating. She pictured him standing at the table, puttering, smelling the same smells she was taking in now. It was easier to talk, picturing him like he had always been before. He felt accessible.

"I want to tell you that it's okay. Zia told me everything. I know you made mistakes. And I'm sorry that you were never able to put things right. I remember, you know. I remember that summer when I came home, how I couldn't sleep at night, how I would walk by your bedroom and I could see you, outlined in the dark, sitting on the edge of the bed, lost in thought. I should have asked you what was wrong. Why sleep couldn't seem to find you. Maybe you would have told me. And I would have told you, too, that you didn't have to worry, because, see, I wasn't motherless, not for a moment. I guess it's true, what Sira says, that we're somehow shaped by the memories of those we love, but I think that it is then up to us to decide what to make of ourselves. I came to Italy because I felt lost. I don't know what I was looking for; whatever it was, what I actually found were stories. Stories like these." She placed one finger gently on the crumpled paper. "I met people, new people and people I'd known before, in this new place. I saw statues of goddesses, ruins, odes to lovers crumbling into the sea. I rode a horse, and people shared their food with me and showed me their land and their love. I saw anger, frustration, and love and determination, sometimes all on the same day. Sometimes in our very own family. You know what I want to tell you?"

The tears were coming now, fast and hot, and she did not feel ashamed of them.

"I know that it's a changing world, papà. I know you wanted to protect me from it, from hurt within and hurt without. But I need to learn to look at *all* things. Including what isn't pretty. I've started writing again, Dad. I'm going to stay here, at least for a little while. Don't worry, I'll transfer my credits over and keep going to university. But I'm going to write a little piece for a local newspaper, and I'm so excited and nervous, and I know that means it's the right thing to be doing. I wish we could talk about it, because I want to write about you, one day. I want to write about your country. If you were here, I would tell you about what I saw, and I would say, papà, I think Italy is an artery. Jarring in its incredible ability to become lifeblood not just for the people who are from here, but also for those who only come for a little while, or who have never been here at all but dream of it nonetheless. If Italy is blood, then it is the vibrant color of that which has gathered oxygen and will sweep from the heart to the entire being. An arterial nation. What do you think of that? Then I think you would tell me to take that thought and run with it, not to close my mind. That everyone can be their own artery. That we are a mishmash of generations, of people, cultures, all thrown together into this concept of globalization, and sometimes we elbow each other while trying to find a place to set our feet down. And then I'd say, Dad, we deserve to be better, for each other, for ourselves. And you'd laugh at me from your great height and say, how, Little? And I'd answer, papà, I think the trick is in taking the conversation from war to peace, not just big wars and big peace, but even little wars and little peace. Take the conversation to what's important: human beings and their stories, their own and the millions that intertwine with theirs. We could make a rule: that you could never hurt what someone else loves. And everything, every*one*, is loved by *some*one else. It must be that easy. It would grow from there."

She was hiccupping now, the words a torrent. "So, as I have a right to my arterial nation, then you have a right to yours. And if we realize it's all the same blood, then… maybe we would be more careful of how every piece of string adds color to the whole."

She looked around the room, almost expecting a response. Everything was quiet.

"I miss you. But you know how lucky I am? I feel loved. Turns out that's my homing signal after all."

One last thing. *"Ti voglio bene."* And that was right, too. Little turned and switched off the light. The room plunged into darkness, and although

191

in any other circumstance she would have fled the lack of light, in this moment she felt comfortable and safe. She slowly rolled the garage door closed, listening for the clang that would confirm it had shut properly. Then she walked up the walkway to the main house to look for Sira.

Afterward, sitting in her room, Little took her father's stories, his own fragments, and she put them in with her own papers, the questions she had thought only *she* was asking, handwriting to handwriting, creaky penmanship carved with ink on paper pressed against her own crisp printouts and scrawling hand. They looked right that way. She could not make it simpler, or more complicated, than that.

Chapter 29
Sperlonga. Present day.

When Little found Sira, she was holding a piece of paper, smoothing it out with her fingers. She looked almost nervous, then folded the page deftly in half and handed it to Little, who took it, perplexed, automatically scanning the page to see whose handwriting it was. She was surprised to find that it was Sira's.

Sira shrugged delicately. "I'm not the letter-writing type, you know. But I thought we should start a new tradition with letters, a better one. Betty told me that she talked to you about my youth. There were some things I wanted to say, too, and I thought I'd write it down. So here it is."

~~~

Dear Little,

There was a time once, now separated by many cycles around the sun, when I allowed my strength to be taken from me, where I lost entire years for the sake of an ideal that I had built in my head. I wanted to leave postwar Italy. I wanted to fall in love. I wanted to have a family. I thought that this was done in certain, logical steps: that if you marry A, then B will follow, and then inevitably C, and that somehow those letters together will make you feel happy and complete.

So, when he came along, he was my ticket out. He fit the bill. He made sense and oh, Little, I did love him.

Happiness is the thing most worth seeking, but there is no price high enough for that which is our own: our minds, our ability to place our feet squarely on the ground and say, this is where I stand. That piece of time was taken from me, or I gave it willingly out of my own naïveté, but once I realized I was losing myself, it was not the same between us. When I retreated, I did so to preserve the sanctity of my sense of self, of presence, a token I was not willing to give to have access to that world.

No, it didn't ruin my life. Why on earth should it have? When I needed to leave, I left. Sometimes you need to know when is a good time to leave. And then you do. And when you do, you never, ever look behind you, not even once. Yes, you should absolutely put your whole heart into everything you do. But if you realize you put your whole heart in the wrong place, then you need to be brave enough to take it all back again. All of it. Don't leave pieces of it behind, Little, or you'll be chasing them backward for the rest of your days, and I raised you better than that.

Of course, I don't think I would have found myself *without* that particular experience, either. It started my traveling days. I moved away from Italy, and I thought I would never come back. The universe had other plans, lots of them, but I didn't know that then. I've seen the world. Taken the train through the deserts, cut my way through the jungle (which was most inappropriate for a young lady in those years, I can assure you). I've shared meals with princes, explored the Alps and their borders, walked the streets of San Francisco, gotten lost in the market riots of Casablanca. I earned the rights to my opinions, so I never apologize for them. And then I came home. The only reason I stopped flitting about is because my bones are too old now. And so I fear I did this to you, too, Little. Made you a wanderer.

If the things that others have followed have led them to palm trees and swaying beaches, then the truths I have tracked have led me to the Argonauts, to the chill of the water and breath steaming in the air, looking for something lonely and not easily found. Though I may have toasted to turmoil, I have never contended with that which is empty.

Do you remember your high school junior prom? You put on that red dress that took so long to choose and did your hair, took care with your makeup. You've never been fussy that way, and I could tell that you were uncertain. You looked in the mirror shyly when you were done, as though you were just meeting yourself, and when you spotted me in the doorway behind you, you said, "I look nice?"—just like that, with the end turned up; a question. I was worried that you were actually asking if maybe tonight you were worthy of the attention of other people. I don't know if you remember, but I told you that you looked divine, which was true. What I wanted to say was that you are worth empires, planets, swirling stars and gauzy milky ways. You are worth thunderstorms and summer breezes, gentle and much needed. You are worth whispered truths and laughter yelled into whipping wind, the heady breathless feeling at the top of a mountain. And you are worth those things always, in an exquisite dress or in your sweatpants, because it has nothing to do with your accessories or how much weight you've lost or gained, if your polish chipped or your hair isn't the right shade of blonde or blue or green or pink. It has to do with your bursting heart, the kindness you show people whether you know them or not, the way you step out of the way when walking down the street to avoid disturbing birds picking seeds off the ground. It has to do with how much you believe, how hard you try for yourself, whether or not you get back up when you've been thrown to the ground. Do not mistake me: You have every right to feel beautiful in a dress, and I hope that you will have many opportunities for that satisfaction, too. It is just that I wish for you to feel beautiful always, everywhere, for all the many happy hours of a long and magical life. If I have one wish for you, Little, that would be it: that you never, ever feel anything but magic.

I told you that I had made promises to your father about taking care of you. That's true. But I would have taken care of you no matter what, Little. I love you. That has always been my real promise. And I'm proud of you every day, proud of the flight path that you are carving out *for yourself*. I never needed to worry at all, did I?

Your Aunty,
Sira

~

So Little and Sira sat on the porch of the house that Little's father had built, and Little told her Sira all about her adventures and the people she had met, the places she had seen. Her long fingers played through her hair, rested on her lap, splayed out in front of her when she was describing something funny, and then once, for more than a moment, rested on the shoulder of the woman who had raised her, and she said thank you. Some other things, the ones she was not yet ready to say out loud, she left as a note on Sira's pillow, in honor of their new tradition. It read like this:

~

Cara zia,

There were once two birds. One was meant to grow to be of great size and colorful plumage, and one was known as only a common bird, small and quick and neutrally shaded, perfect for the large formations that fill the sky. The little one was determined, and the great one lucky. But then, the colorful bird could not fly, and when she could not find her food, the little bird scavenged it for her. And when the little bird hurt her wing, it was the colorful bird that covered her with her plumage every night, so that the little bird could heal in a kaleidoscope.

My name is Little, because this is what you call me. Like the countries I was raised in, I'm just looking for myself, my own place, while also keeping close all that I hold dear. If I have found the strength in my legs to leap, it is because I was loved, and told that I can fly.

There were once two birds, and that which seems simple, sometimes is the most hard-won of all.

Thank you for telling me stories. About Italy before, and about all of us, my family. Thank you for coloring it in for me.

I do love you so, Aunty.

—Little

Fragments from the Belpaese
An article by Little (pen name), contributor to the Florentine Gazette

When I was asked by my good friend Marta to write an article for her beloved local paper, my hands trembled. I wanted to write about a country, the love of which I have recently rediscovered, and I wanted to write about how powerful we have been made today as individuals. I thought that these were two separate concepts, but as I sat down to outline what I wanted to say I realized that they don't have to be; in truth, they tie together like shoelaces. I wanted to be able to discuss these ideas with people and then I realized this could be the perfect forum, to use today's gift of instantaneous connection to start a conversation. So please, if you'd do me the honor of reading, then let me know what you think. Your thoughts. I want to hear them. I want to learn.

Some say the unification of Italy was completed in the year 1871, when the city of Rome became the capital of the Kingdom of Italy. Rome, whose curse and gift is that she is simultaneously more squalid and diamantine than any city has a reasonable right to be, a city in a country that perhaps has always been this way. Most of us look to 1871 as the official year, although the unification of Italy as a reality is something we're still waiting for. Some days it feels like we're walking backward, and sometimes it seems we catch the scent of the first steps in the right direction. Countries, like people, cling to life chiefly by their resilience, changing direction a minute from the edge, surprising everyone—themselves most of all. Even the greatest contradiction can find its way, and, after all, what peoples are as comfortable with contradiction as the Italians?

Think about this: For thousands of years, we've been able to write. For hundreds of years, we've been able to take pictures. Then we gifted those pictures with movement, to feed our hunger for creating a bond with each other, for sharing. Humans have been expressing themselves for as long as we've been standing up straight, exploring and noting and pushing boundaries.

Some things you can't help. Or save, or make better, or make not have happened. Some things you have no choice about. But some things, some things you do have a choice about. Some tales, you get to write. And, well, now you not only have words, a camera, a pencil, a canvas, a message, a hope, a blank sheet of paper. Now you have the power to spread your message instantaneously, and your audience can be everyone in the connected world. What you have to say today can spread like wildfire. How many people in the past would have loved to have just a shade of this potential for influence? The farthest corner of this round planet is in your living room. You know what the Milky Way looks like, what black holes do to the universe, the sound of the deep echo of the songs of the whales, the explosion of stars. You can reach out and touch all of it, you know exactly where you stand inside of it.

We can talk about Italy, the country whose borders we have left repeatedly, determined never to come back; yet we always do wander back, even if only when we wake with a start in the middle of the night in a place far away, with the sounds of Rome fading in our ears. I want to write a love story, of Italy today and Italy yesterday—and a wish for the Italy of tomorrow. My father once said that we have the right to express disagreement with something, but that we then have a duty to be part of the solution. So if we, whether that is today's up-and-comers or the generations that were young before us, want to change the direction we're going in, we need to step up and step in.

There is no excuse anymore for not going out there and chasing down your dreams, no room left for no room. So take those pictures and post them, record those videos and hit that upload button, write down those thoughts and put them online. Embrace what you want to say and define yourself by being someone who also embraces what other people have to say, even if (especially if!) their words, hopes, dreams, fears, and loves do not coincide with yours. We have become truly powerful beings. And the attention goes wherever we choose to direct it.

This is a story for the third generations (the fourth, the fifth, the sixth generations), for the not-so-lost generations, for the hybrids. For the people who feel more at home in an airport than they wish they did, who yearn for one place to call home but also always, inevitably, long for something they do not know, miss places they have yet to behold, people they have yet to meet. This is for the ones who have grown up checking if the gate has changed, who have both struggled with and embraced transience, have learned to find themselves in the moments in between, that have found a place to belong in the very unbelongable (I just made that a word). This is for the ones who always say goodbye, who have learned too well how to keep tears from falling until they've gotten through Security. The ones who cry inconsolably when they get on that plane but are always ready to say hello on the other side. For the ones who hear the sea even in the rumble of the 747 as it wakes up, who have chosen freedom but know that they have placed their roots everywhere, not nowhere. Everywhere, in the laugh of the friends they never forget, in the people who wait for you at Arrivals even when your flight is nine hours late and you stumble off the plane in the middle of the night during a thunderstorm. Lifetime friendship, your blood runs in my veins friendship.

So. Mix your colors until you have the shade you've been hunting for, choose your words carefully, walk out to the very edge, and say quietly (you don't need to yell, we can hear you), I'm here, too!

For the ones that see Rome everywhere they go—or Tunis, Gubbio, Dublin, Aleppo, Santorini, San Francisco, you name it, it's yours. You bring your home with you.

There are stories, and they are everywhere. Empty pages full of possibility, futures to be written, worlds to be dreamed. Stories upon Stories, all waiting, patiently, to be told. Until one decides it is time, and jostles to the front, trembling. My turn. Tell me.

THE END

Acknowledgments

I've been wanting to write an Acknowledgments section since I was a tiny girl who dreamed of writing a book, so of course, now that the time has come, I'm really just worried I'll forget someone incredibly important. If you're that incredibly important someone, you're already in the second book. I actually just wanted to surprise you!

We are, I believe, ultimately as great as the people that inspire us; they set the distance between us and the stars and, if we pick really good ones, they nurture us so that we know there is no such thing as distance. If I had initially thought that this book would be a solitary process, it was because I hadn't yet realized that, like raising a child, it takes a village. So, here goes:

To Maryna Taran, my partner in crime in absolutely everything, from books to work to long conversations about *The Witcher* and life. You are brilliant, and fierce, and I am in awe of you every single day. Thank you for reading, and re-reading, and re-re-reading Little's story with never a word of complaint.

To Evacheska DeAngelis, who has been my best friend since she walked into art class at Dominican University of California almost fourteen years ago and realized that I did not know then, nor would I ever know, how to draw a cup, and that if she did not step in there was a very real chance that I would fail out of Intro to Drawing. We've never looked back. Thank you for your expert eye and fierce support during this years-long process, weeg.

To Jennifer Lewis, for her infinite help with all the matters of this book, from reading new iterations to discussing illustrations to simply being there. You are the best thing that Young In Rome brought me.

To Miranda Pantano, my besty, for reading my manuscript even when it was still a compilation of stories that didn't know how to fit together, and for believing in it since then. And to Sabrina Pantano and Marie Coluccio: your endless love for Italy, and the stories that were both your own and of your families, stuck in my head and planted the ideas that ended up being this book. What would I do without you, my tribe?

To Melanie Dimstas, Hiwot Thompson, and Claire Spadafora, all of whom have either read different versions of this book and/or displayed infinite patience when I woke up at 4 a.m. in a bronchitis fever haze and texted ten million subtitle options (Mel). And that's just the beginning. I have been blessed not just with friends, but with sisters. You powerhouse women never, for one second, allow me to give up on myself. How does one say thank you to those that have taken your dream in their hands and helped you mold it and breathe life into it, simply because they love you? I am blessed, and I am honored.

To Caitlin Foley, true warrior princess, who even while adventuring in Saigon sat down and texted with me about cover background colors for an hour. I can't wait until the next time we get to sit and drink *prosecco* together and cry over the beauty of Pat Conroy's writing. I'll try not to crush my fingers in the sliding door of the bathroom next time.

To Laura Tognoni, who sat with me over breakfast in Bodrum one day, being kept from her lounge chair by the sparkling cove in favor of helping me pick out Delila's storyline.

To Olivia Flynn (and her scrappy sidekick Harissa), Liam Arne (my favorite Thai food thief), Susan Nelson, Camille Coquoz, Mae Deevy, Eric Buckmeyer, Dario Anelli, and Mathilde Vaultier, all of whom gave kind, thoughtful insight on image and wording choices. I have the mightiest friends.

To Marta Laurienzo, who continually, through her own actions, shows me the type of woman I want to be, both in my career and personal life, and who told me over lunch at Red Café one day that I should never,

ever give up. I remember your words, always, every time I fear I may fall.

To Marianne Ward, who never fails to be there, no matter how busy she is, whether I need help picking out a quote or help figuring out life, and who knew when it was time for me to leave the nest, even though I was terrified my wings wouldn't hold air. If I flew despite my fear, it is because you believed in me so utterly that I believed it too.

To Laura Lo Cicero, confidante and dispenser of the best advice, the first person there during the beginning of an adventure that is still going on today.

Per Anna Maria Palmieri, che ormai, più che amica, è diventata famiglia. Per tutte le conversazioni dove mi hai ispirato a continuare a scrivere questo libro, per tutte le volte che hai creduto in me quando non credevo in me stessa. Cosa farei senza di te?

To Bjarney Friðriksdóttir and Eva Ng'inja Croft, my Tunisia family, for always being there when, in the middle of the night, I want to know which line, color, or font you like best. Even though we're all in different parts of the world now, the sisterhood remains exactly the same.

To Ducky, who is always in my corner. I can't wait to see what the next pages bring us.

To Barbara Colaiacomo, Flaminia Scarcella, and Alessandro Matta, my Expedia guardian angels. You guys believed in me at a time when I felt lost and very little, and you made working with you feel like home. I'll never forget it.

To the team at Ali Ribelli Edizioni. Thank you, thank you, thank you, for taking this dream and making it something real, something tangible.

To Michele Rubin, Managing Editor extraordinaire of Cornerstones Literary Consultancy, and Dina Rubin, the best proofreader in the world. What a mighty duo!

To Catherine Michele Adams of Inkslinger Editing, without whom, truly, this book would have been an entirely different story.

To Gabriella Contestabile and Francesca Belluomini, two astonishingly talented authors whose beautifully written words and support have moved me to tears on more than one occasion. I am honored to count you both as good friends. You ladies show me the very great strength to be found in women supporting each other. I am so excited to see where our Italian trio takes us.

To Katerina Miras, graphic design wizard, who took my idea of turning Young In Rome into Which Way to Rome and made it burst with color, imagination, and the perfectly drawn Vespa.

To Cinzia Bolognesi, who graciously turned her (incredibly talented) pencil to creating the book cover, map, and images you find inside this story. Thank you for bringing it all to life.

To Laura Fabiani, superwoman owner of iRead Book Tours and Italy Book Tours, who reached out to me several years ago to see if I might want to write book reviews for her company. I did, and Laura, since then you've become not just a friend and an inspiration, but someone I deeply trust in all matters literary. Thank you for your advice and support whenever I send you emails with the subject along the lines of, "I have no idea what to do".

To Corrado Maria Daclon (Fondazione Italia USA) and the inimitable Michelle Fabio, who also wrote amazing testimonials. Michelle, your writing and verve are of such inspiration to me. The fact that you took the time to read through All the Way to Italy before it was polished meant the world to me. Thank you for your words.

To the wonderful Young In Rome/Which Way to Rome readers who took part in the subtitle contest: the fact that you cared enough to take time out of your busy days to provide feedback and be a part of this process makes me deliriously happy and grateful. I hope you guys like the book.

And to Mr. Richard Ragan, who, without knowing the reason I needed a quote, graciously helped me pick one out. And who, in November 2017, had our office watch the documentary *Finding Joe*, which turned out to be exactly the infusion of courage I needed at the time.

Almost lastly (but never leastly), per mia Zia Gina e Zio Rolando, per Zio Gianfranco, e per Nonna Isolina e Nonno Pietro.

E per mio papà. I hope you're smiling from up there. I hope you're saying, "I told you so."

Biography

Born just outside of Rome, Flavia Brunetti grew up bouncing back and forth between Italy and California, eventually moving back to the Eternal City and confirming her lifelong commitment to real gelato. Flavia holds a Master of Arts degree in Government and Politics from St. John's University and a Bachelor of Arts in Political Science from John Cabot University. Today she travels the world working for an international humanitarian organization and spends her free time writing and wandering around her beloved Roma in constant search of bookstores and the perfect espresso. You can find her city blog on Rome at whichwaytorome.com and her portfolio of published writing at flaviinrome.com.

@whichwaytorome

Published by Ali Ribelli Edizioni
www.aliribelli.com
redazione@aliribelli.com

CPSIA information can be obtained
at www.ICGtesting.com
Printed in the USA
LVHW111115200219
608131LV00006B/79/P

9 788833 460581